ALEXANDER KOROTKO

BERA AND CUCUMBER

BERA AND CUCUMBER

by Alexander Korotko

Translated from the Russian by Michael Pursglove

Proofreading by Stephen Dalziel

ALEXANDER KOROTKO

BERA AND CUCUMBER

TRANSLATED FROM THE RUSSIAN BY MICHAEL PURSGLOVE

GLAGOSLAV PUBLICATIONS

CONTENTS

MASYA

Solomon Volkovich Nukhlis was slightly if solidly built, fairly well-fed, and penguin-shaped. He always appeared before a potential client suddenly and decisively and, without giving him time to collect himself, took the offensive and struck a swinging blow to the weak spots of the possessor of his imminent advance. Solomon Volkovich juggled the words "old age" and "solitude" like a professional juggler tosses firesticks in the circus ring. It was precisely at these historic moments he would take the bull by the horns and drive him mad.

His arsenal was full to the brim with a variety of verbal psychological weapons which, so our hero firmly believed, left his victim no chance of refusal. The start of the attack depended not so much on the personality of the repentant as on the dark areas in his biography.

The following recitative was offered to persons whose income was dubious: "Don't think you're the cleverest and that no one will guess where you got it from, what and when." And then in a softer and trusting voice: "Oh, stop it and calm down. I'm not after it." And his ward, who lived in perpetual terror, didn't hear the second part of the monologue and the first acquaintance already seemed far from the first, and he felt himself to be not on the threshold of his own house but in the dock.

After his preliminary bombardment, our hero would retreat exactly three paces from his opponent, get a none-too-fresh handkerchief, wipe the sweat from his brow and, without allowing his partner to collect himself would leap abruptly, boxer-style at his opponent, insofar as his belly allowed, and would exhale sacral sounds which, like oxygen, filled his balloon-like words with a particular symbolic sense.

Thus was born a part of speech in the form of a chain of, at first sight, meaningless sentences. Here is one of them: "How can I know that you don't know. Don't compel me to persuade; it won't help."

Yes, he loved Alexander Blok and Andrei Belyi and considered himself to be their successor, but this was a secret hermetically sealed and hidden deep in his soul, like the heart of Koshchei the Deathless.

When the session of simultaneous playing with the nerves and emotions of his opponent was drawing to a close, he was waiting, not for the ovations but for the transformation of his client into a customer. However, there were occasions when his client, now recovered from his delusions and in a semi-conscious state, would try to the best of his ability to slam the door in his face, but to no avail – a size thirty-seven foot stood like a latch in the doorway. Sometimes the client, instead of shaking hands on a deal, missed the opportunity – *oy vey*[1] – and the Broker (thus Solomon Volkovich styled himself), would get it you know where, and why, but we won't talk about that.

The image of our hero would not be complete if we didn't mention the main feature of his character – his good-

---

[1]   Yiddish: phrase that expresses grief, pain, or frustration.

ness. In fact, he was only sharp and impulsive with insects; with people he was accommodating and tactful, soft and indecently ingratiating. Admittedly, a client's reluctance to be happy would cause bursts of rage in him and he would become hysterical, but this would last only a few moments and was more like flashes of lightning during a thunderstorm.

As a rule, clients did not notice these cataclysms on the Broker's face; they were more concerned with their own worries. Our hero would quickly suppress his anger, his blood would return to its usual channel and the conversation would continue smoothly along shores named in honour of buyer and seller.

Solomon Volkovich always dreamed of being a philosopher-philanthropist, and even a patron of the arts. He had a hankering for the carefree life of beauty, but the wind of change blew him off course and he would sit on a sandbank in the inshore waters of unsettledness until the night breeze of success remembered him and bore him away to other shores, where there would be no grey weekdays or queues, where the handout in the form of a pension would find itself a new victim. His best years went by in expectation of this. Were they the best? It depends what one compares them with; but there was nothing to compare them with.

Thus he lived – not so much through memories as through the hope that one fine day everything would change. He even imagined how burdensome luxury would become and the idle chatter of models who sought intimacy with him. At such moments Solomon Volkovich experienced not so much an excess of strength as a sleepiness and depression; he couldn't stop yawning; his imagination painted cheerless pictures of his future life, satiated and monotonous; he wanted to abandon everything and get the hell out of it. Then he bethought himself and realised that he was at home anyway and his life, ruined by desires, was on duty, like a sentry, preserving his present from the nomadic raids of illusions.

Usually such moods took hold of him deep into autumn, when the mahogany buds of sunset were swelling. He dismissed these delusions, as he would have dismissed importunate flies and swiftly, stepping out like a soldier at a military parade, marched past the rostrum of his solitude and went to work, as if to war.

"After all, the most important thing in our business," Masya never tired of saying (this was the affectionate name given him by his late wife Mirra) "is mood and the certainty of achieving your planned goal." Truth to tell, he realized no one was waiting for him anywhere. No, well so what? He didn't land on their head like snow and after all, snow has the capacity to melt. Solomon Volkovich was more like a tick – if he attached himself to you, it was for a long time.

Masya, forgive me for my indelicacy, but he considered himself to be to some extent a Messiah; true, not such a big and real one, who would come and save the Jewish people after its victory over Gog and Magog, but a modest little one, like David, conqueror of Goliath; but all the same a Messiah. After all, when a deal went through, he rescued, he dragged from the abyss of solitude aged, weary people.

Yes, Masya was afraid of everything on earth, but this was only the outward manifestation of his character; in his heart he was a wild beast, a gambler. As far as courage went – *azohen vey.*[2] Sometimes nuances let him down – but

....

[2]   Literally translates as "when [I want to say] 'oh' and 'vey'." "Vey"

whom don't they let down? He only had to take a deposit and come to an agreement with a customer about setting up a new family nest when one of the doves (his name for the future loving couple) would, for no particular reason and, so help me if I tell a lie, without informing him in advance, depart this life. But Masya was no mystic and did not expect to return and, terrible to relate, did not believe in the resurrection of the dead. You will say: but he still got the deposit. Yes, he did. But Masya was not a man to be satisfied with little.

But how so? The reader may be outraged, and with justification; after all, our hero, like his clients, was on his own. Why did he not think of himself in the first instance, being the owner – don't misunderstand me – of the oldest profession. The fact is, he was, by nature, fiery and passionate, frequently got carried away, and in a way he at times dealt with others, could allow himself, who was far from being a stranger, to be palmed off, one never knew when, with goods long past their sell-by date – as they say on the Moldavanka, to create a right *tsuris*[3] for himself.

When he wasn't earning his daily bread, or to be more accurate, dosh, he could sit for a long time on the deserted seashore and gaze into the distance. The events which were happening behind the scenes of the horizon afforded him no peace at all, "Theatre is theatre," Masya muttered continually, "and I know its *foyle shtik*[4]." Passers-by thought he was thinking "for eternity." But he didn't in-

means "grief," and "oh" expresses a sorrowful mood with moans and sighs.

[3]   Yiddish: a difficulty, trouble.

[4]   Yiddish: monkey business, underhandedness.

tend to lift a finger in its direction. With his range he wasn't up to mountain heights.

When you looked at Solomon Volkovich you began to understand that everyone, bar solitude, repudiated him. He had not lived out his time; he had avoided it.

But something unusual had happened in every year of his life. That's what happened this time too. A feeling of his own worth overfilled him and the joy of existence poured over the edge, and it was, of course, summer, when Masya rented out his dacha with board and lodging at Bolshoi Fontan 16th station. Well, what do you mean, he hadn't done anything for a long time, for anyone else; of course, it was for himself. It was a time when Solomon Volkovich pushed the boat out, and not just one boat. As they say, *mazel tov.*[5]

Can a confirmed bachelor feed himself three times a day? It turns out he can, but only in summer and only at Bolshoi Fontan 16th station. The morning would begin with a celebration; breakfast was merely the cause of everything. Our hero would go out onto the terrace, where there was an old, high quality oak table, wearing wide flannel trousers, a white linen shirt, over which were decorative *nepman* braces; on his feet were white canvas shoes. A real king, somewhat powdered with mothballs, but a king all the same, or, as they say in Odesa, *yurets.*

At table he was thoughtful and magnanimous, as was appropriate for the heir to the throne. The picture was slightly spoiled by his retinue, that is to say the flat dwellers who were indelicate enough to sit alongside him, but in spite of this, he was affable and indulgent and gave no indication that this circumstance had hurt his pride and gave him

---

[5]   Good fortune.

no opportunity to spread his wings finally and soar to the mountain heights, where his chaste soul, an equal among equals, touched the wellsprings of his past life and did not wish to return to the cage, to the physical envelope named Solomon Volkovich.

These were indeed tragic moments, when he hovered between life and death. He had one soul, a real smasher, but what about his body? A pitiful sweet wrapper, nothing more. All the same, these were incomparable moments of bliss; in our hero spiritual insight would open out, he would be possessed by prophetic visions, his hearing would react to the smallest sounds and whispers. He would hear the voices of his forefathers. The only thing he could not distinguish was where the voice of Abraham was, and where Isaac and Jacob were. He wanted to betray his country and settle in the Promised Land and, standing at the Wailing Wall, to atone for his sins. This access of incandescent passion reached its apogee and Masya would rise like an eagle, higher and higher and, when he reached the sun, would burn his wings and fall like a stone to earth, where the cares and anxieties of a new day awaited him.

As you have already guessed, the events about which I want to tell you, took place in summer. It was holy August in Odesa, majestic and impressive. When a melancholic breath of wind merely disturbed the mental equilibrium of its citizens, Odesites did not move, expecting changes, and prayed for mercy. The houses with their wide-open windows reminded one of hatchlings in the nest with open beaks, eager for coolness, as if it were manna from heaven and it came closer to dawn in the form of a draught which roamed from the kitchen to the bedroom, from the bedroom onto the balcony, and the heat of the day, the fire-breathing dragon Zmei Gorynych, would back off and return to its native penates, to the steppe, and there wait until midday when it would regain its power over the city.

At this lifeless time of year Nature was heavily pregnant and had no time to think about such trifles as coolness, and Odesites guessed this and did not grumble and, indeed, why grumble when everything breathed delight.

But the sea, what about the sea? It lay breathless, lower than the level of passion and contemplated the sky with colourless fish eyes, in the mirror of its solitude. It was a different matter in winter. The sea and the steppe, torn apart by jealousy in the horizontal plane of love, tormented the town from all sides with dank winds which penetrated the soul and the unsubjugated town was reminiscent of a fortress and endured siege after siege. Well, what can one say apart from, in a word, Odesa is a hero-city.

One has only to start talking about Odesa before one loses the thread; you want to phone someone, agree to meet them, whizz off at breakneck speed to a café, hang around the town aimlessly and, totally exhausted and scarcely able to move one's legs, return home, settle in front of the television and think, not about a better life, but about how splendid it is to do nothing.

But it is time to return to Solomon Volkovich.

Like every solitary person, our hero had his quirks which, with the years, became less attractive and more prominent. Undoubtedly, these are expenses, so to say, the consequences of his beloved brokerage business, And what's so surprising about that? Every profession, with time, puts its stamp not only on a person's gait, on his behaviour, but also, most importantly, on his character. After ten years working in a school a teacher shrieks like a half-slaughtered piglet, not only in the classroom but also on public transport, in the market and at home. An experienced psychiatrist can, with a good dose of conditionality, be termed, mentally healthy.

How the brokerage profession was reflected in Masya – you can't tell at first sight. Although there was a feeling he had grown tired of struggling with his obesity. But something else scared him. Loneliness and old age skipped after him from morning till night, as if pursuing some down-and-out who had stolen a piece of kosher pork from some honest tradesman. But he did not intend to come to terms with these gerontological ailments. Masya had decided to try on the role of madman, not *of gantse kop*, that is to say, not completely off his head, but just a bit. Whatever it was it was a diversion. In his heart he was not simply an actor, but a mega-actor! It cost him no effort to convince himself that his reason had given way by force of circumstances.

But the important thing was that others should believe him. And what do you think, they did! From that moment began a process of reincarnation à la Stanislavsky. His head, overburdened with thoughts felt sufficiently wise and independent of the opinion of others. He was not immediately aware of his greatness. At first his consciousness was subject to annexation – and off it went, off it rode. In the end he grew quite accustomed to the role of wise man; his speech became more measured, more persuasive. So, in any event, it seemed to him and he had grown used to trusting his feelings. Already Masya was not speaking, but prophesying. Not only adults, but adolescents and even children had begun to make quiet fun of him.

He was born, and grew up, on Malaya Arnautskaya Street, and his whole life had passed in full view of an old Odesa *dvorik* or yard. Solomon Volkovich was the image of a wise man twenty-four hours a day, so it was impossible to catch him out. His neighbours thought he had gone in the head, though admittedly not very far. But no one doubted he was heading that way.

Rumours of his greatness quickly took on flesh and began to circulate not only in the familiar yards, but on the streets of the Moldavanka. Adolescents even invented a game called "I'm listening to you." That was the first phrase that issued from his lips when young people turned to him, ostensibly for advice. Those of them that were granted an audience during the day would gather in a neighbouring courtyard in the evening and would take a vote to decide which story of their encounter with the wise man was the funniest. The winners got a bottle of port, the losers chipped in and together they would drink the winner's prize. Everyone was happy, especially Solomon Volkovich.

Weariness, sleepiness and other adjuncts of age vanished, old age and loneliness retreated for a while and awaited the return of their attenuated high point. The role was a huge success, but he wanted more. The Broker's secret dream was to be reincarnated as King Lear, but there was already a whiff of real madness about that and he decided to bide his time with that role. However, events had no influence on the timetable of Masya's life. He was a pedant, and that says everything. He brought together not only two ends but lonely people as well. Every one of his clients was making his own way to loneliness, to that point of inevitability where the boundary between the present and the future was obliterated, and only force of inertia allowed them to get through the wilderness known as the day.

Loneliness is an uninhabited island, around which there is no one for thousands of kilometres. No, of course there are people, but they exist in parallel worlds. Imagine the Eiffel Tower or the Leaning Tower of Pisa standing in your yard or growing in your garden, like the Tree of the Knowledge of Good and Evil. It was to such an island that Solomon Volkovich came and, like Father Frost, distributed presents in the shape of hope for new life. Masya paired his doves, adhering strictly to a rule devised over the years: to rich, prosperous grooms he offered modest, materially challenged brides, and to well-to-do young ladies, grooms with no income at all.

If someone ventured to ask why this was so, what, as they say, the *tzimmes* was, he would reply irritably. "Who stopped you studying physics at school?". And would add, with an intelligent expression on his face and guile in his eyes: "Like charges do not attract but repel." Such an approach produced results, otherwise he would long ago have put his false teeth on the bookshelf where Blok and Belyi stood.

And something else about perhaps the most important secret of his career. This should not appear cynical to you, but Masya was convinced that every real broker should have his own Koreiko[6] – his millionaire backer. The mere thought of this prototype made him younger, more mobile and more energetic. No, he was not greedy. In recent times he had not avidly sought wealth; he wanted to create a fund

....

[6]   A reference to *The Little Golden Calf*, a satirical novel by Soviet authors Ilf and Petrov.

for the defence and support of lonely and impoverished people. This idea had totally taken over the consciousness of Solomon Volkovich and already he could think of nothing else. There were moments when he wanted to forget about his profession for ever. His broker's wheeling and dealing lay on his soul like the heartbeat of minutes and drew nondescript pictures in his imagination. Here he was, no longer a broker, but a raven flying home to his courtyard on Malaya Arnautskaya and being driven away by both adults and children. The past day seemed uncomfortable and lopsided and more like an abandoned and rickety peasant hut with a leaky roof and gaping black holes instead of windows. Something wrong was happening to him again.

Milky rivers of fog were carrying Masya away to the summit of an active volcano of doubts. A fiery lava of conscience flowed down the slopes of his presentiments and en route burned down the bridges which linked his past and future lives. In the pre-winter exclamations breaking out from the old haunts of the foliage he could hear the cry of his soul and he flew after the foliage to another life, where the Sea of Evil and the Sea of Good eternally swap places.

He began to think seriously about taking up permanent residency in Israel, where Sonechka lived, his and Mirra's only daughter. Sonechka had been inviting him over for a long time, complaining that his two grandsons had got out of hand, since she and her husband were out at work all day. Masya even went to the Israeli consulate in Odesa, completed all the emigration documents and even bought a one-way ticket. But he decided not to take this step.

Reflections about the Promised Land exhausted Masya. He found breathing difficult and perspiration covered his brow. Masya felt a slight tremor in his hands. Without realising it, he halted in the middle of the avenue; the ground began to give way beneath his feet... Fortunately there was a bench nearby. Masya perched on the edge of it and suddenly, in this deserted spot, an unfamiliar voice rang out:

"What's this stupidity?"

"It's not stupidity," Solomon answered into the void, in no way surprised.

"Don't play games. Give a straight answer as to what doesn't suit you."

The dialogue was taking on a harsh character, but this did not faze Masya at all. On the contrary, he was unspeakably pleased that for the first time in many years he had met a worthy interlocutor, albeit an intangible one but nevertheless an interlocutor. He had long wanted to sound off; it was just a pity that the theme was the most painful one for Solomon Volkovich. But what can you do...?

"So where was I?" said Masya aloud, apparently coming round. "Oh yes, about Israel."

In reply a familiar, but irritated voice rang out, a voice which brooked no contradiction.

"Why do you harp on about Israel, Israel! You're not going to Sinai but to see your daughter. Don't forget that. And what keeps you here?"

"Mirra's grave, and freedom. I don't want to embarrass anyone, not even my daughter." And, drawing breath, Masya added: "Understand this: grown up children have to be loved at a distance. That distance guarantees that our parental feelings grow stronger year by year. In fact, not only I need it, but, above all, Sonechka and her husband Fima need it. What's more, I'll be a fish out of water there. Parents and children should live apart, and this isn't a theory but an axiom. I'm surprised I have to prove this to you. The exodus of the Jews from Egypt happened fortunately, but my exodus from Odesa – alas, no. Let's drop the subject for ever."

Solomon Volkovich bowed, did a U-turn and, his shoulders drooping beneath an insupportable weight, set off on his final journey towards loneliness. And so, in his effort to achieve once again the goal he'd given himself, he set off home.

Opening the door, the key to which hung on a rusty nail in the door surround, in full view of everybody, Solomon Volkovich passed through the neglected bachelor veranda, hurried into a cold, orphaned room and immediately cast a glance at the old, creaky bed. Under it, in a cardboard box, in which a puppy had once lived on which he had taken pity and picked up in the street, was kept his sole, and main, treasure – his archive. Unlike Chichikov's dead souls[7] these were living histories and the fates of living people.

A few words about how the archive arose. When acquiring a future client was in the offing, Masya, as a genuine intellectual, did not contemplate his pocket. Come on, he was above that. Yes, he wanted historical truth, but his methods were of an exclusively humane, scientific nature, and he would begin by unearthing the CV of his subject. As a passionate archaeologist of human temptations, he was interested in every artefact. His broker's tactfulness did not allow him to invade the spiritual sphere of his guinea pig; he limited himself to the exclusively material sphere.

The research part of his preparation for the meeting was the most important fragment of his work and afforded him huge moral satisfaction. Perhaps this demonstrated innate

---

[7]   A reference to *Dead Souls*, a novel by Nikolai Gogol.

curiosity, but in the language of Solomon Volkovich – amateur photographer of thirty years' standing – his stage was called "sharpening the image."

As soon as the Broker crossed the threshold of his flat, he first locked the door, padlocked it and chained it and, without undressing, like a real scuba diver, he dived under the bed with a lighted torch between his teeth. What new could he find in his card index? But there's nothing the Devil doesn't joke about, and the Devil never jokes.

Masya convulsively leafed through the out-patient cards of his clients; he had adapted these for his card index, and suddenly, between the third and fourth exhalation and inhalation his eye fell on a completely unfamiliar card bearing the totally unusual name: Ivanov. How could this have happened? After all, he not only remembered every client by name but also every detail about them by heart, like children of school age learn poetry. Masya not only did not believe his eyes, he did not believe the circumstances or the place in which he found himself in the role of scoundrel. Doubts began to creep into his head: had he confused the address and the flat? And, if he wasn't in his own home, what if the real owner came any minute?

"What can be done?" Masya kept repeating through parched lips.

"Nothing can be done." This was the familiar voice of either an invisible man, or simply a spirit.

"So I'm at home?"

"Yes, not only at home, but under the bed."

"Phew," said a relieved Masya, but all the same he didn't believe it.

He decided to crawl out and satisfy himself personally that this was his flat and that everything was in place. He rose to the surface, looked around and finally convinced himself that he was at home. He had to go back. And, once again with the torch between his teeth, Masya dived to his former depth. Under the bed, like a coral reef, stood his hoard, but now he was interested in the form bearing the concrete surname: Ivanov. Before taking it in his hands, he pinched himself painfully on the cheek. This was sufficient and Solomon Volkovich began to acquaint himself.

A former director-general of the Secret Research Establishment "post boxes," general, professor, Hero of Socialist Labour, member of the regional party committee, deputy of the last session of the Supreme Soviet of the USSR. Yes, with a CV like that it would be possible to implement Masya's dream of creating a fund and of greening the desert. Without realising it, Masya, faced with the general's distinctions, stood to attention, admittedly in a horizontal position and closed his eyes in terror. A profound dream came over him then.

Before him stood the figure of Ivanov, wearing a general's uniform. Without ceremony he ordered Solomon Volkovich to report to him the following afternoon. He was to report fully how work was going on the creation of a fund for lonely and impoverished people and whether the object would be achieved within the planned time schedule.

While the general was issuing instructions, Masya carefully scrutinized this colourful figure. General Ivanov was solidly built, some two metres tall, with a shaven skull and arms reminiscent of sledgehammers. On his forehead was a large wart which resembled a ladybird.

The general disappeared as quickly as he had appeared. With an effort of will Masya raised his eyebrows, which reminded one of iron roller shutters in an expensive boutique and, afraid to move, peered into the darkness. But to no avail; under the bed was quiet and damp, as it had been before the general's appearance. After such a visitation it made no sense to be afraid of anything and the Broker crawled out with difficulty, pushing the box of forms in front of him like a trolley.

Sitting at his table, he wrote out the general's address and began to prepare himself for the following day's meeting. A heavy, sleepless night had fallen. Finally, the most important day of his life arrived, Masya changed the habit of a lifetime and ordered a taxi.

The general, as one might have expected, lived in a secure elite settlement. How could it have been otherwise with such a CV? But when the Broker drove up to the designated address, unforeseen complications arose. There was a barrier across the entrance to the settlement, and security men immediately approached the vehicle. One of them took a look at the taxi and at Solomon Volkovich's outward appearance and contemptuously asked a completely tactless question.

"Who do you want?"

"How do you mean – who?" The Broker met question with question. "The general, of course."

"Which general?" the security man persisted.

"Ivanov, of course. Who else?"

The answer was not encouraging.

"There's no one lives here of that name."

Masya not only sank deep into the car seat – his friable body took on the shape of the seat. At that very moment in the control point where the security men of the elite settlement were stationed, the phone rang. One of those on duty took the receiver, briefly answered "Got that," raised the barrier and came up to Masya and said:

"Go through. Monastyrsky, Naum Markovich, is expecting you."

"What Monastyrsky? What Naum Markovich?" muttered Masya perplexedly, with ill-concealed irritation.

To which he received a more than convincing answer.

"Don't fool with us. Go through."

And so it was that the taxi drew up to an opulent detached house of improbable dimensions. On the terrace, amid quivering birches and against the background of a lake sat Comrade Ivanov eating a *bublik*[8] split horizontally into two halves and covered with a thick layer of butter. A samovar was steaming on the table, lump sugar lazed in a sugar bowl, next to which were sugar tongs and a cup of hot tea.

But the householder was not drinking tea out of the cup, but out of the saucer, slurping and not hiding his pleasure at the whole process.

Ivanov greeted his guest offhandedly and invited him to the table. Masya went up to the terrace and froze rooted to the spot in front of the general. He could not believe his eyes.

"That's needed." The only phrase spoken was not said but exhaled and hung like a cloud between the Broker and the houseowner.

Both the head, bald as a billiard ball, and the sledgehammer-like arms, and even the art on the forehead – everything came together. Solomon Volkovich was taken aback. They contemplated one another, not as enemies and not as friends, but as people spellbound.

....

[8]   It is a ring of yeast-leavened wheat dough, popular in Eastern Europe.

An inquisitorial silence took hold of Masya's plans and thoughts; his head was ringing. It wasn't the sound of the sea, but of time, which had stopped and was slowly evaporating, like tea from a saucer. The silence was abruptly broken by the general.

"Why have you come, who invited you and what do you want?"

Like the striking of a gong, these words brought the Broker out of his stupor and he began the fight with Goliath. The infantry went into action, then the cavalry, then the artillery. As they say, the whole arsenal; and even the Supreme Command reserve. Ivanov did not interrupt, but nor did he listen.

Masya's last words: "What are you thinking of? Are you not ashamed to be alone? Do you want to live until a time when there'll be no one to serve you a cup of tea?" compelled the general to stand up.

Solomon Volkovich fell silent. He had the feeling that he was standing at the foot of Everest and couldn't see its snow-covered peak, that is the head. He had never before felt himself to be such a repressed little being.

"Solomon," said the General in an already more emollient tone. "Was it not you a long time ago?" Then he added more pointedly. "But why is there a button missing from your jacket? Was there no one to sew it on? But you went on about getting married, getting married, so don't make me laugh."

He seized Masya by the scruff of the neck, as one seizes a kitten, and, placing him on his knees, began to stroke his head, as if he were a child. As he did so he said:

"Don't cry. Don't shiver, I won't hurt you. I've heard, and I've read in the paper, that you want to set up a fund to help lonely and impoverished people. Well worth it. I'll help you. I've got good friends who I think will agree to join me in investing money in this noble enterprise."

He sat Masya down opposite him and covered him with a plaid.

"That's better."

The Broker no longer believed his eyes, nor yet his ears. Our hero realised that if he did not contribute to the dialogue at once, he'd be thrown out like a kitten.

"In actual fact I…"

"What do you mean 'actual.' Let's talk turkey."

"All right," Solomon Volkovich replied bluntly, in masculine fashion. "Who are you actually and what's your name?"

"Come on, come on, make him breathless," an inner voice whispered to Masya. "Just so," said Masya, answering his own question, then saying, much more decisively:

"You're an Ivanov with a nose like that?"

"I can see you're not the timid sort," replied the general, stammering and now without metal in his voice. "You see, my friend, life makes adjustments to our calligraphy. Yes, the ghetto's been abolished and they've taken a five per cent cohort of Jews into higher education. So it's not clear what's better – for there to be a ghetto or for our faith to be stronger. I know one rector who said I'll only take Jews into my institution when hairs sprout on my palms. And me? What am I? I'm Monastyrsky, Naum Markovich. I was Ivanov in Soviet times, you understand, on the Nationality line of my passport. Once I was summoned to appear before the regional party committee and told: if you want to grow, change your nationality and your surname. So I became a Russian, Ivanov, and then director-general of secret research establishments and a professor, a Hero of Socialist labour, a member of the regional committee of the party, a deputy of the Supreme Soviet of the USSR."

"Yes, I know." Masya addressed himself in some irritation and uttered the secret phrase which he'd had on the tip of his tongue all the time:

"How do I know all this?"

"That's not my concern," replied Naum Markovich in an authoritative tone, adding "*bikitser*[9]. Get to the point. I'm offering you the post of president in the newly created fund; I'll choose the chairman and members of the board of directors. As you yourself realise, these must be trustworthy people. That's agreed then. I'll give you a lawyer. Prepare standing orders and a constitution and register the fund with the executive committee. As I promised, there'll be start-up money. So good luck, former broker."

On this lofty note they parted.

Life whirled and spun with unbelievable speed, reminiscent not so much of a carousel as a Ferris wheel. Masya could no longer distinguish day from night. Everything went smoothly. The fund was registered within a week. The City Executive Committee of the Party passed a resolution to sell to the fund, at residual value, an empty twenty-two-apartment block built in 1907, on Preobrazhensky Street. In no time at all the fund's building had been restored and now resembled a palace. The citizens of Odesa rejoiced. The listed building was resurrected, like a phoenix from the ashes and, alongside the opera house became one of the main sights of the city. For the president of the fund, its founders acquired an executive

....

[9]   In Odesa, it means "make it quick," "very quickly."

Mercedes and a penthouse in a historic part of the city, with a view over the sea.

In the course of a month the team was fully constituted. Speechmakers, image-makers and stylists worked on Solomon Volkovich's image. The former broker was dressed by the most expensive fashion designers in town. A pool, a gymnasium, masseurs and cosmeticians did their bit. Masya seemed about forty years younger. No, that is no exaggeration. To convince yourself of the fact, look at the stars of show business. Fifty years ago they looked much older, and our hero is no worse than them.

It really does happen like that: one person and two lives – one big past life and another little real life. One thing today, another thing tomorrow, but between these todays and tomorrows lie, not twenty-four hours, a standard day, but a chasm. So what is it that nevertheless links them, these different shores, islands, planets and even continents? Could it be the righteous life, the desire to live a better life, violent passion, a favourable wind of change and, perhaps, will power, but whose? The Creator's, of course. It is not us but He who chooses and sends prompts in the shape of stories, one about Cinderella, another about the fisherman and the fish.

And Masya? What about Masya? Everything had come to pass; he was inaccessible. And he was happy? How can one know, as long as he doesn't open his heart? We won't know, but he did give cause for envy this way, that way and the other way. Let's begin, perhaps, with Malaya Arnautskaya, but here everything is different, my friends. People were proud of him there; after all he was one of theirs.

Half a year went past. He was standing on the penthouse terrace wearing an expensive suit and a snow-white shirt, looking at the sea. It seemed to him that no one in the world felt the sea like he did. As he looked at the raging element, Solomon Volkovich suddenly realised what was happening in his soul. Maybe the sea was his soul and he himself was nothing, dust, a hollow being, an empty one-room flat lacking furniture, comfort and warmth. But the sea seethed, changing its colours and shades, summoning help. But how could he save both his soul and himself? Again he wanted to look beyond the horizon and see, beyond the fiery red curtain of the sunset scenes of spiritual life, but his imagination failed him. From the height of the spiritual bog all that could be heard was the croaking of frogs in the subterranean underpasses of satiated normality.

Masya took himself in hand, looked nervously at the clock and left the flat. A company car was waiting at the door, with a driver and a security man.

Throughout this whole period of transformation he had not seen the general once, nor heard from him. The impression was formed that the meeting with Ivanov under the bed on Malaya Arnautskaya Street was nothing more than a mirage, a *fata morgana*.

Which general could this all be about, if Masya could not recover his sense – he had got lost, had forgotten his past life. Our hero was more like a sick man who had undergone a major heart operation and even clinical death, and the action of the drugs had been so powerful it had completely deprived him of memory. But after a time he began to distinguish objects and to evaluate events which happened not only to him, but around him.

It turned out that the whole fund team had been taken on without his agreement. When he tried, delicately, to clarify the situation with his chief deputy, the man replied, in no way embarrassed, that the directors had delegated staffing matters to the supervisory boards and that he, Solomon Volkovich, was here, to carry out their wishes and receive a handsome salary and dividends.

Solomon Volkovich found it really difficult to envisage his life without a company car, elite housing, expensive restaurants, trips to Europe and other trifles which embellished the life of a lonely boss. There was neither much money, nor little money but there was enough for everything. He simply spent it easily, like a darling of fortune. But who in their right mind would refuse such a life, Masya persuaded himself.

But of late, persuasion had not helped; something had cracked within him. It was like a chiming wall clock; the clock hung there, as it always had, but the chimes were inaudible and time began to limp round the dial, to be minutes slow from life, then hours slow, and, at any moment, to stop altogether. "If only this hadn't happened to me," thought Masya, realising that you won't get far swimming against the current – you'll drown.

Solomon Volkovich heard a voice he'd long since forgotten: "Take your head in your hands, or what's left of it, and key in at least some logic, if your brains aren't working." And Masya engaged reverse gear, remembered his profession and his wretched past life, full of discomfort and dignity.

From that moment he began to study carefully every financial document he signed, and not only that. Day after day he reconstituted events which had happened to him over the preceding half year. Now his huge study, with its rest room and reception room, including the penthouse, had shrunk to the dimensions of the dark room where he had once developed his photos. "Yes, I can see you're no fool," a familiar voice said late one evening, "you've nevertheless collected a picture of your past mosaic." Masya was impatient to pose a single question to his unknown friend, but he'd not managed to utter what was on the tip of his tongue when the voice said:

"You want to ask where I've been these six months?"

"Y-yes," replied Masya, stammering slightly in his perplexity.

"Where I've always been."

"But why didn't you open my eyes earlier?"

"I spoke, shouted, even sent you a text, but you were deaf and blind. Alas, that often happens to people. You're not the first, or the last."

"What's to be done?"

"Just don't ask me daft questions. What's to be done? I've got a Herzen too. Or ask me who's to blame. Go and get ready for a meeting with the general."

And so there was Masya on the familiar terrace. The same samovar, the same sugar bowl with lump sugar, the sugar tongs beside it and the *bublik* split horizontally into two halves and covered with a thick layer of butter, the cup, the saucer of tea resembling a smoking volcano and waiting for the general to moderate its heat with his breath and at the same time warm his cold soul.

It was early spring. April, untouched by the heat, seemed like a noble young knight, ready to come to one's aid at any minute. A gentle sea breeze was fiving a fencing lesson. Well then, it was time to start the duel.

The general looked tired; his pale face spoke of a sleepless night, maybe more than one. But Solomon Volkovich was in a determined mood and did not allow his heart to show pity. Ivanov-Monastyrsky spoke first.

"I know, I know, my friend…"

But the Broker did not let him finish. He didn't intend to defend himself and launched his attack.

"How could you have acted like that with me, and who gave you the right? No thanks! You thought I wouldn't make anything of your machinations and that you would exploit me to the limit?"

A smile, more like a scar, appeared on the face of the general.

"That's what I thought, and not only thought but did actually do. I made one mistake: I didn't suppose you would come to so quickly. I thought we'd cooked up not a bad deal on the quiet; in exchange for your chaste soul I gave you material benefits and a pretty comfortable life. I even covered your back to a certain extent – all dubious operations were given to the chief deputy to do and, as they say, in case of dire need, included it legally in his functional responsibilities."

"I've found Mephistopheles," snapped Masya.

"Not at all, it's just that I've read Chekhov carefully. You must agree that my general, chief guest at the wedding, was much more preferable."

"Robbing lonely and impoverished people – is that not the height of cynicism?"

"Allow me to say I didn't take a kopeck from any of them. I simply took advantage of your idea and ardent nature. What's bad about that?"

"It turns out you're not only a cynic, but a bastard too. How much money do you need to finally calm down?"

"Don't you see, for me money isn't measured by amount. For me it is the sole source of energy, the equivalent which I find essential to support my vital functions."

The conversation had hit the buffers. The Broker was nervous. As at their first meeting, at the crucial moment the general had seized the initiative.

"Stop!" screeched Masya in the total silence, "That won't do!"

He leapt from his chair like a scalded cat, ran up to the general, snatched the buttered *bublik* from his calloused hands and began to eat it frantically.

"Oh, how you scared me. All right, finish my *bublik* if that will help our dialogue. I've got another one," said the general imperturbably.

He took out a lawn handkerchief, blew his nose noisily, and in a delicate manner which was unusual for him, lordly and taunting, he asked Masya how his mental processes were working and, without waiting for an answer, continued:

"Do you think it possible that a man like me could fail to know about your every step? I knew everything, of course. Not only did I know but I also allowed no one to stop you. You will ask why. Because you are a totally chaste person. I'm not worthy of tying your shoe laces. I'll say this too: it cost me no effort, from the first day the fund was operating, to appoint another chairman in your place. But it was very interesting for me to try out a man like you with money, power and other fripperies." At this point the general switched to the formal mode of address. "And you bore this trial and taught me a lesson; not just a lesson – you turned my soul inside out, you changed my life! Before you I could never understand how one could follow the precept of David: 'If riches increase, set not your heart on them.'"

A warm May evening set in unexpectedly. The dissembling moon listened to the birdsong. The silence was frightened with the newness of feelings. The general remained on the terrace. Masya set off for Malaya Arnautskaya…

And yet nothing returneth again according to his circuits. Masya, absolutely happy and absolutely unprotected. Stands at the Wailing Wall. From whom does he need protection, when there is only him and God.

LEVITSKY

Odesa does not demand sacrifices. The doors and windows of heroism are boarded up and you sleepwalk through tunnels of the unconscious in the deaf hermetic space of solitude and along streets of childhood and youth, in the carapace of a lethargic dream of recollections, breathing in the aroma of past life. But alongside are people, many people; they move and orbit, as the Earth does the Sun. You can touch them mentally and even pinch them, but they will not feel any pain – they are from another reality. You will plunge into the sediment of the broth of student life, but even there you are absent.

Whose is this life which seethes, which thrashes about like a fish on ice on the steps of time? What day of the week is it today? Seems like it is the first day – a working day for those around you and a holiday for you. How nice it is to be guest in your own home! Something has gone, has disappeared irrevocably, but perhaps there never was a past life and all your past life is measured by just one day – today. Thus, the past becomes the present.

That which is lost is not only the sole inheritor of past life; it gnaws the soul with enigmatic recollections, and it doesn't matter that it is impossible to mark the boundary between invention and reality. And the further you are from childhood and youth, the more reality becomes an invention and frees you from all responsibility for what happened in the past. Thus memory involuntarily makes you kinder and more romantic and that is the chief virtue of time, which does not want to grow up at all.

Late autumn. I'm standing at the landing place of Kovalevsky's dacha. A mystical panorama of sky unfolds before me. To the right it's like Delacroix's picture *The Paris Commune*, or like the Red Terror in Russia, while to the left it's like alpine meadows of turquoise clouds. Behind my back a stray wind exchanges whispers about something with the sea. And the city, like a cocked trigger, will at any moment fire memories at point-blank range.

Snowflakes, improbably white snowflakes, were not falling but dying in the air, like the cotton wool balls with which we used to decorate the Christmas tree. As a result of the frost our cheeks were like paradise apples, but all this was scenery, a prelude to the main event of winter – gliding smoothly downhill on home-made sledges, to which, for greater speed and to make them run better, instead of the usual runners, circular steel pipes were attached. At that time, how I pitied adults, boring, worried adults, deprived of the possibility of enjoying the winter fairy tale!..

I was so buried in my memories that I didn't notice that I'd arrived at the hotel. Suddenly I felt someone behind me twitching the hem of my coat. I turned round but there was no one beside me. However, I'd not gone more than a few paces towards the hotel when the twitching started again. It reminded me of fishing when the goose quill float tells you that a fish is beginning to take the bait and will soon swallow the hook. Feeling myself to be both the bait and the float at the same time, I could not make any sense at all of what was happening to me, but the fact remained: I continued to be pecked at surprisingly insistently, like a bait. But maybe the fault lay with my sickly imagination which had led me to persistent hallucinatory comparisons with fishing.

While I was frantically seeking the cause of what was happening, I was seized by the sort of panic not normally found in pedantic people; an inner voice yelled at maximum volume: "Do something." So I did. Once again, but more abruptly this time, I did a 180-degree turn. But, alas, once again I was disappointed: not only did I find no one near me, but the side street in which the hotel stood was also deserted and lonely. I looked at my watch. It was one fifteen in the morning. Absolutely devastated and crushed by what had happened, I went back to my room, took a sleeping draught and fell asleep.

In the morning I decided not to think about what had happened to me, and began the day, as usual, with a swim. There was no one in the pool, and I revelled in the solitude. My body found its equilibrium and my soul, which had been out of sorts since the previous day, regained a state of peace. I deliberately did not try to look at my watch. Firstly, I was in no hurry to go anywhere and secondly, I wanted to be in a state of physical wellbeing as long as possible. After all, I wasn't in the least bit tired. Tiredness would come later, but would only add new colours to acute sensations.

At some point the pool began not to be mine alone. I left it with gratitude and, once in my room, realised that I'd swum further than usual today. Not that that grieved me; it was simply that recently I had categorically refused to hurry and was prepared to be late, to the detriment of my habit of punctuality. But today was a special case in that it involved the hotel breakfast. I did not want to deprive myself of the pleasure either of excellent food, which at my age was of some importance, or of the atmosphere in which I had immersed myself and in which I felt comfortable.

I'm even afraid to describe my feelings, so as not to dissipate that spiritual state which had made me an invisible man. At those moments everything was subordinate to my imagination. I took advantage of this without ceremony, even abused it, but tried very hard, by the end of breakfast, to return to the body which had been cast to the whims of fate, to breathe life into it and begin the existence of an ordinary person.

I made a very strenuous effort, collecting all my will power in a fist and appeared in the restaurant at my usual time. Already over breakfast it seemed to me that the hotel staff, including the waiters, were giving me peculiar looks. Surreptitiously, so that no one suspected anything for long, I looked at myself in a mirror. This was not difficult to do – there were mirrors everywhere. I saw nothing unusual about myself, apart from dishevelled hair and a guarded look, but knowing my tendency to hypochondria and self-criticism, I had no doubt I would not calm down until I got confirmation that everything was normal with me. As if reading my thoughts, the woman in charge of the room approached my table somewhat uncertainly and tactfully asked: "Is everything all right with you?" "Yes, quite all right," I replied nervously, "but what's happening to you? Maybe I should call the manager." Not expecting this reply, and totally discouraged, the woman began to justify herself, saying she had not wanted to cause me any inconvenience in any circumstances, or to place me in an awkward position. "It seemed to me that you'd been upset by something and I thought that it might be connected with your stay in our hotel." Then I realised how tactless my behaviour had been; I apologised and the incident was closed. As I left, I suddenly saw this nice young girl standing in the corner and weeping. I felt ashamed. In general the day had not worked out. I realised that the main culprit was the state I was in as a consequence of my adventure the previous day. But was there a boy?[10] That was yet to be elucidated.

After breakfast I decided not to go back to my room. There was no sense in staying between four walls. I went out into the city. It was a typically dank autumn day. Not a trace remained of yesterday's hospitable Odesa. And that wasn't surprising. It seemed to me that, in some mysterious fashion, the state of alarm had been transferred to today's weather, and I saw nothing unusual in that. It seemed to me that an overcast cloudy sky was a mirror reflection of my inner world; how else could I explain to myself the alarm forming in my soul since yesterday and with the commotion in the sky since morning, or maybe, not since morning but from the very moment when I was visited by other-worldly forces.

A plot. But where did I get that from? I don't know, but the word "plot," as soon as I uttered it, began to revolve on my tongue like a spinning top. Plot, plot, plot…No, it was too much. In order to get out somehow, to swim out of this whirlpool, and so that this vortex did not drag me to the bottom of amnesia, I decided to switch my consciousness from what was going on in the labyrinth of my emotions

....

[10]   "But was there a boy?" is a reference to *The Life of Klim Samgin* by Maxim Gorky; the speaker doubts that what happened to him last night was real.

to an external irritant and to observe what was happening, not with me, but around me. I immediately dived out of the orchestra pit of my presentiments, transferred to the stalls and began to observe with great interest what was happening on the stage of life. This allowed me for the umpteenth time to convince myself that life is nothing but a theatre and we merely the audience and nothing more. I surmised that there are members of the audience who are not only good actors but who, divorcing their "I" from their essence, look at themselves from the side; that is to say, they are simultaneously actors and audience. But for the moment this was too much for me.

And so, I was in the theatre. The final bell had rung, the lights had gone down and the performance had begun. Primorsky Boulevard served as scenery. The two protagonists were Pushkin and Richelieu. They had different roles but what united them was the fact that throughout the whole show they didn't let slip a single word. It would be interesting to know who the author was of this production. But I'd completely forgotten – of course, it was time. But I won't get distracted by the heroes. Even without them there was much that was comical happening on the stage.

Here was a solitary old woman sitting on a bench, feeding bread to the pigeons. Alas, one could not say that she was enthralled by this; there was in her eyes so much tragedy and solitude that the sky seemed to weep as it looked at her. It was impossible to go past without pain in one's heart. A little further away a homeless person with improbably kindly, tired eyes had found a place on some sort of mat. In front of him stood an empty beer can and, without speaking, as if wanting to emulate the protagonists in the play, he was begging for alms. Beside him sat a dog, the only living thing devoted to him. As a sign of gratitude for every donation the dog barked. When I put in a couple of coins, the dog, scarcely audibly so as not to attract the attention of passers-by, quietly bared its teeth and looked me in the eye. Its look was amazingly touching and full of despair. Its whole appearance gave one to understand that it felt horribly awkward – not for itself, but for its old friend. What else did I manage to read in its eyes? They said: "Don't think badly of him. He was very trusting, and his nearest and dearest, when he fell ill, cleaned him out of everything. But we mustn't feel sorry. Simply try to understand." Whether this was a gesture of despair on its side, I don't know. I only know it was like humility.

I was about to go on my way, in the direction of the Potemkin Steps[11], when I caught a look from the same old woman. She did not conceal her envy of the homeless person – she would like a dog like that! After all, her children had given up on her long ago. She had forgiven them long ago but was constantly worried about them. After all they didn't know in what direction life turns at times, especially when kindness deserts the heart.

But the show continued to follow the planned scenario. A couple in love now approached the audience. In the gait and gestures of the young man could be detected a spoiled but highly talented artist. The girl did not simply hold his hand in hers but pressed up against the strong figure and was afraid to miss any word. She did not simply love, she revered; after all, she too was an artist and who better than she could appreciate the genius of her friend. In general he paid no attention to her, simply weighing

....

[11]   The Primorsky Stairs is the historic name of the Potemkin Steps.

and savouring his every word. He needed the girl. Thus, a temporary halt, he needed to fill the pause of solitude with someone. His tragedy lay ahead; it would become really big after their separation; the wound called first love would be cicatrized but would never heal, but that was a scene from another show.

I had not even noticed how the first part ended; I went out into the foyer, drank a bottle of champagne and, wanting to continue, ordered another two bottles with some embarrassment. At that moment the third and final bell rang and I took my place in the stalls.

But newer and newer characters were appearing on the stage. Who amongst them was positive, dammit? Surely the director hadn't kept them for his own admirers. And now there appeared on its trainer's shoulders a talking parrot; it did not simply talk but entered into dialogue and even tried to discuss. I decided to play my part, went up to the parrot and spoke first: "Well, then, my beauty, how's life?" "What do you think?" the parrot answered at once. I was stunned, but, as they say these days, this forced me to engage with my opponent. I immediately countered that life is life and must be accepted for what it is. "I see you're a philosopher. No, I'm wrong, you're just a layabout and a whinger." The parrot had begun to annoy me. Be that as it may, the most unpleasant thing was that around us had gathered, or, to be more precise had flocked, a crowd of gawping onlookers who were observing our exchange of fire with unfeigned interest. I was in a quandary. At any moment I wanted to send the parrot on its way and for me to go my way. And thus I would have proceeded, if the parrot, *a propos* of nothing, had not said, with a touch of irony or sarcasm: "Don't do yourself down, I was joking, you're a splendid fellow. It's just that I've been in a terrible mood since yesterday." At that point I could bear it no longer, and asked: "Really? You too?" "And what do you think? Parrot or man?" After the conclusion of our dialogue, people began to disperse, realising that no scandal had come about. As a parting gift I patronisingly, mentor-like, clapped the parrot's owner on the shoulder. What a shameful end to a stroll!

In point of fact the trainer and his parrot should have clapped me on the shoulder – saying "good health, mate." After all we didn't give away either your terrors or your weaknesses, nor yet your inner disorganisation, but simply let you go free, like a bird is let out of a cage, realising that you, like the bird flying out of its cage, would, once free, come to grief. After such insight I again felt completely apprehensive and shattered and decided to go back to the hotel in the hope of managing a few hours' sleep.

In my room I plunged into a chasm of solitude. Enclosed space always had an oppressive effect on me. It could be compared to the reaction of my liver to alcohol. My liver was unforgiving about evening imbibing – in the morning it would reply not only with a headache, but with growing depression in the shape of a tsunami of bilious forebodings and a terrible mood. Nevertheless I fell asleep, maybe from nervous exhaustion, maybe from the weight of events that I had yet to go through. I entered sleep as one enters the open doors of a summer, unrestrained and unprotected from the transience of time.

…Here I am with Senya Yukhtman and Kolya Levitsky – yes it was the same Levitsky with a left wall eye. What are we about? What time of year is it outside? Summer, of course, school holidays. We make our way surreptitiously to Michurinsky Gardens, in order to steal as many green peaches as possible with youthful fluff framing the oval of these as yet unripe creations. Out of fear that the park warden would see us and fire his Berdan rifle, loaded with salt at us, we acted like barbarians, convulsively ripping the peaches from the trees and stuffing them down our shirt fronts. Our trousers, held up by military belts, retained the stolen peaches in our tee-shirts, which became reminiscent of shopping bags. The stolen booty made our chests and stomachs burn with a bright flame as if sunset had emerged from the shores or as if we were undergoing the terrible tortures of the Inquisition and were wrapped in red cloth. But stolen goods never bring happiness and the peaches hidden under the bed never ripened or matured. But that was what happened to Yukhtman and me. Levitsky's peaches which were also hidden under the bed, in an aluminium bowl, turned into magical southern delicacies. We couldn't believe it – they were like rosy-cheeked transparent white *naliv* apples. Why on earth did our peaches rot and Levitsky's ripen?

I woke up. My left hand was clutching a ripe peach, just like one of Kolya Levitsky's which I'd seen in my dream. I decided to eat it, to convince myself that a dream is a dream, but reality is reality, and had nothing to do with anything that had happened to me before I woke up. I attacked the peach greedily and convinced myself that not only was it fresh and juicy, but also amazingly sweet.

In my mind I again returned to Senya Yukhtman and Kolya Levitsky. The three of us lived in Odesa, on the Moldavanka, had been in the same class in secondary school no.21, behind the Starokonnyi bazaar and we really did run to the Michurinsky Gardens to steal "shaggies" – that was our name for green, unripe peaches. But after we left school, we lost one another. Does that mean that everything I saw in my dream was the truth? How could I forget? Kolya Levitsky really did treat us to peaches from the Michurinsky Gardens. At the time I didn't attach any significance to this. But the fact of the matter is that at the beginning of June there were no ripe peaches either in the Michurinsky Gardens or in the whole of Odesa. Then I remembered one detail. Unlike Yukhtman and me, after the Michurinsky Gardens, Kolya did not complain about getting an itch from the skins of green peaches. But could that have been so important then?

In the last twenty-four hours I had already looked at my watch several times. It was just after three. Not having any plans, I left the hotel and wandered round the streets of Odesa, wanting to bring nearer the time appointed for our meeting. What nonsense was this? What meeting and what appointment was I talking about? What on earth was I doing talking to myself, not at all embarrassed by passers-by and not concealing the irritation in my voice. And for what reason did I have to wait for a non-existent meeting, in a non-existent place, at an unknown time? Don't try to be clever, you know very well that, not far from the hotel, at 23.00 this meeting had to take place. Who on earth are you intending to meet and who told you that it would take place at 23.00 just here? Well, this is precisely the place and the time where this story started yesterday. And who are you about to meet? If only I knew? Well. Yes, it's not important. Don't bother me with stupid questions, I don't feel well as it is. You'd do better to tell me how to kill time. What's this I hear? You want to become a killer and have decided to take me on as an accomplice? You'll get nothing out of this. I can only be a witness. And in actual fact, who are you? I am you and you are me. Do you mean to say that I have a split personality? But why do you latch onto words? Split does not mean a split…If you want me to go then say so. No, what are you doing? Don't leave me alone. I don't intend to abandon you. I simply won't become your second I, but you. You'd better not anger me. Forgive me, I got het up; you can see that I'm out of place. How's this! He feels out of place because he's claiming mine. But I'm not claiming anything; I simply wasn't ready for such a development, my thoughts, my presentiments became confused, and, what's more, this post-prandial dream knocked me out of my stride. I need to calm down. Not you, but us. You again want to drag me into a discussion? Surely you can see that just a little more and I will lose control of myself. Look how soft we are! Why did you come to Odesa then, so many years later? I don't know. Wait a minute. A day before my arrival I had a dream, or perhaps it wasn't a dream, it's difficult for me to say. No, I remember exactly: it wasn't a dream – visions simply flooded over me in the shape of pictures from my childhood, when, at my grandmother's in Korosten, I and my peer group would run to Bazaar Square to watch them putting up the Circus big top for forthcoming performances. After these visions the light went out in the hall of my imagination and I returned as if nothing had happened to my everyday activities. The day was long and rough – one event was succeeded by another and each new event supplanted the preceding one. It goes without saying that in my long-term memory they were preserved, as if on a hard disk otherwise how could I have reproduced events from two weeks ago? I don't know about other people but I consider myself an events psychopath. I need something to happen to me all the time, otherwise the sharpness of my perception is blunted, a beam falls from my eye and I sink into depression. And how do you get out of this state? Very simply: I change the picture of the reality surrounding me, that is to say I move from one place to another. And does that help? Of course, it's my only means of salvation. I seem to be beginning to get to the truth of what happened to me that day. It was as if had begun to go into another spin and this vision, like a medicament, saved me from depression and I, like a bird, flew out of the cage of reality and here I am in Odesa, perching on a branch of memories and chirruping with you. Is that not too many enigmas for the last two days? The visions before my journey, the happening yesterday evening and today's post-prandial dream. I don't know – perhaps these are all links in a single chain, but I feel that an answer is not far off.

I had to think what to do next in order to untie this Gordian knot. I decided to turn up, as I had done yesterday, alongside the hotel, at the same spot, and at the same time; and for the umpteenth time I looked at the dial. There were five and a half hours until the appointed time. I at once decided against returning to my room, as that would be an absolutely unacceptable variant. Instead of that, I indulged in my favourite occupation of wandering through the familiar streets. But everything turned out to be more complicated than I thought. Suddenly a simple truth was revealed to me: if your soul is unquiet, any activity, even if it distracts you from nagging thoughts, immediately makes your favourite activity your unfavourite.

I began to count the expensive foreign cars driving along the streets. At first it seemed that everything was going fairly smoothly, but I quickly grew tired of it and saw that it killed practically no time at all. It even seemed to me that time had stopped, had decided not to move, in order not to be distracted and together with me had taken on a more useful task – counting cars.

I cannot say that everything that was now happening to me, did not excite my imagination. I have to admit that I am a venturesome man, but that's only one side of it. On the other, I loathe vagueness or situations when you suddenly find yourself in a dead-end. In such cases I take only one medicine, the name of which is intuition. I rely completely on trying it out, but in order to effect a complete recovery I take my courage in both hands, stop the headless chicken routine, stop panicking and wait for the signal. It will definitely come. The main thing is not to switch on logic or common sense but simply to trust in the prescription written out by intuition. I realised that this was just such an occasion.

The answer was not long in coming. Why are you making an issue of it? Get on a Number 15 tram, go to the Moldavanka, go into the courtyard where you lived, pass along Poperechny Lane where you spent your childhood and youth, and time will flow by, like a mountain river and the walk will relieve you of your anxiety and agitation, calm your soul, build up your confidence and, full of strength and energy, you will go to your planned meeting you know not with whom.

So here I am, sitting on the Number 15 tram and travelling along a route I know so well. While I travelled the prompting of my intuition could be read like a scrolling banner in my head. It meant that everything was all right – and I got ready for the meeting. And it would certainly take place. I calmed down and escaped from the dead end.

It took place even in the places ground down by my memory. I was surprised that I was not filled brim-full with either delight or disappointment. At these moments I was like a dishevelled sparrow bathing in a puddle of rainwater. Yes, I was happy with that quiet, unconscious happiness which, if it does happen, happens very rarely. In order to touch it, you have to live, as a minimum, a long life, full of drama. My return to my childhood reminded me of the halt in the wilderness by my ancestors, who had come out of Egypt.

The primordial silence of the lane discouraged me. How could it be that in the half century of my absence nothing had changed here; I realised that that could not be so, that probably everything is possible if belief in it is impossible. I went, like Gulliver, along this toy lane, past crooked, ram-shackle little houses and measured my past with the paces of recollections.

It was only here and only now, being in this geographical spot, forgotten by civilisation, that I suddenly – not simply keenly – understood, to the point of feeling pain in my temples, but felt that all my triumphs and acquisitions were of interest to those who did not wish me well or envied me and were of absolutely no interest to me. Such are the twists and turns of fate! It was necessary to return to one's past in order to witness the collapse of the Babylon of one's own illusory achievements. I found it impossible to understand why, finding myself two paces away from my own house, not only did I not approach it, I made no attempt to have a look into the courtyard. Something was stopping me and that something came from the realm of the subconscious, and not only from there. But to the end I did not want to admit that to myself.

The start of the eleventh hour of the night. It was time to return but time underwent remarkable metamorphoses. As soon as I got to the Moldavanka, time not only progressed round its orbit, pausing at each number, it began to go past at unbelievable speed. I hesitated, but made up my mind and swiftly, so as not to think too much, went down the sloping earthen embankment, flung open the familiar wooden wicket gate – and there I was in the courtyard. At one point it even seemed to me that I had simply forgotten the existence of the house where I was born, as if someone from on high had switched off my consciousness at the moment of my appearance on the Moldavanka and I had become a controlled drone. Of course, it was difficult to think up some big idiocy, but I had not got much time left to fill the blanks in my memory.

The next event was no less strange. My watch still said it was the start of the eleventh hour. That meant I had been here more than two hours. Unbelievable! And I felt that I'd not spent more than a quarter of an hour here. Clearly something was happening to me. I was even surprised that in such a state I more or less adequately evaluated what it was. It seemed to me that I'd already gone through a gate which I'd known since childhood; however, at the same time I was standing on the mound in front of my house, which meant I'd not entered the yard. A delusion!

Determinedly casting aside all doubts, I went down to the house along the earthen embankment trampled down by the decades and cautiously, even uncertainly, opened the gate I'd known since childhood and with difficulty squeezed myself into the narrow passage between the fence and the house. The old fence divided the yard into two unequal halves. If one ignores the dimensions of Israel and Palestine, everything else, including the essence of the conflict, was analogous in nature. But, in contradistinction to the countries of the Middle East, here the two sides had never had diplomatic relations and did not support terrorism. They simply lived peacefully and quietly hated one another. Next door to us lived a nurse, Nina, who never thought about who had what nationality and, to the surprise of the opposing side, treated me to hematogen[12]. But once she said: "Things are quiet with you Jews," at which point her face became covered with red spots.

And so I'm in the yard. It was dark. There was no light showing in any window. I suddenly felt I was not in Odesa in the yard of 17 Poperechny Lane, but in Egypt, witnessing the ninth plague which the Almighty inflicted upon the pharaoh and his people "and there was darkness over the land of Egypt, a darkness which may be felt."

But the darkness in the yard treated me kindly – made me less vulnerable and more confident. I began to penetrate the depths of the yard. The move turned out not to be of the easiest. The thing is that the configuration of the yard and the fence had an ill-defined geometric form. To get out of this tunnel and into the open I had to go to the end of the block and, as soon as I saw steps on my right, in front of the entrance – there were exactly three of them, it meant that I had overcome all difficulties and reached the main square of our yard. True, it lacked a Triumphal

....

[12]   Hematogen is a nutrition bar which is often considered to have medicinal properties, and is used to treat low levels of iron (e.g., for anaemia); it was very popular in the USSR.

Arch but it had a puddle in the middle which never froze and never disappeared.

The neighbours had dreamed up the name "main square," having so designated the widest place in the yard – from the wall of the prostitute Sima's house to the fence. The covering of the yard was highly intricate: along the wall of the house cobbles had been laid, although to apply the word "laid" to what the inhabitants had to cope with every day may be described as extremely relative. In bright weather they had the opportunity to avoid stumbling and breaking their heads, but in the evening and at night – alas! The rest of the square was covered with soil over which, selectively and in separate patches, asphalt had been laid, or at least an approximation of it had, more resembling cow pats, but insofar as there had never been cows in the yard, it was unanimously agreed to consider the covering to be asphalt.

The house in which I once lived was the only one in our yard with foundations. The remaining four buildings could only be called houses relatively speaking. They were crooked, jammed up against each other, warming not only their walls, but everything around them. They exuded such touching defencelessness that we were not only afraid to touch them but also to breathe on them. But the most improbable thing was that from these absurd, decrepit and outwardly unattractive dwellings there came forth a mysterious life force, and in this inscrutability, in its genetic code, lay the key to the longevity of the Odesa courtyards.

I grew up isolated. I had no other friends except Kolya Levitsky. He lived opposite our house with his parents and his two sisters in one room on the fifth floor of a multi-family construction hostel. Kolya regarded the world only through his right eye. It was perhaps because of this that he had a rather strange walk. Before he began moving, he would bend his right arm at the elbow to an angle of ninety degrees and turn his body forty-five degrees to the right. His mode of travel was somewhere between a trot and race-walking. Kolya considered that in this way he constructed a car out of his own body, and the right arm bent at the elbow was nothing other than a steering wheel.

How did Kolya fare at school? He didn't. Every term the school council sat and decided to transfer Levitsky to a school for children with learning difficulties, but, for reasons which no one understood, not only was Kolya left in school each time but, most surprising of all, he moved up from class to class. That said, Kolya made no effort to improve his performance. Performance and Levitsky inhabited parallel universes. When this or that teacher went berserk and asked Kolya an elementary question, Kolya, with an absolutely vacant expression on his face, failed to understand. This was occasioned both by the excited state of the teacher and by the heightened interest in his character. Whenever I asked Levitsky why he didn't study, without any embarrassment he would reply: "Why? I know everything anyway." The answer was so discouraging that there was no point in continuing the conversation.

My grandmother, Fanya, was very sorry for my friend and every time she saw us together, she would invite him to dinner. Unlike me, Kolya ate silently and very fast. As soon as he finished eating, he would get up from the table just as silently and leave without saying a word, and I was left to finish my dinner. I could not understand how one could get up from someone else's table and leave without saying thank you, as if nothing had happened. The most surprising thing about this story was grandmother's reaction to his strange behaviour. Every time this scene took place she would say: "Don't blame him, grandson. The important thing is that he's eaten and left with a full stomach." In actual fact Levitsky did not go anywhere; he stood behind the gate and waited for me to leave and play *mayalka*[13] with him or for us to go and play "fires"[14] for money with other boys.

We were growing up. The time came for us to leave school and we were preparing to sit leaving exams. And suddenly, one summer day, Kolya was no longer there. No one could understand where he'd gone. No one found him anyway.

I looked at my watch and was horrified. It was just after two o'clock. I couldn't believe that I'd spent three hours in the courtyard in total darkness. There was nothing left for me to do but to leave this enchanted place and return to the hotel. When I left through the gate it seemed to me that it scarcely creaked behind me. I did not attribute any significance to this since all my thoughts were directed to getting to my room as quickly as possible. I took a taxi and soon was in the centre of the city. Despite the late hour I decided to get out several blocks before the hotel and traverse the same route as the day before. I didn't think this would produce the expected result, but I had to calm down, to cool off. Furthermore I realised that if I returned to my room at once, I would hardly sleep till morning. I walked with cat-like tread, looking round constantly and realising that this looked rather strange from the side. My fears were baseless.

....

13   Once a traditional children's toy, used as a cheap alternative to a ball.

14   A children's game, popular from the 1960s onward, the aim of which was to throw a coin at a small pile of coins. The thrower claimed any coins knocked over.

As I approached a familiar spot linked to the previous day's event, I felt excitement and, as it turned out after a few minutes, not for nothing. So there it was – I froze at the same spot, hoping for the long-awaited meeting. Suddenly I felt I was the subject of burning looks, as if exceptionally powerful laser rays had been directed at me. I experienced a sharp pain, followed by a feeling of being unwell; I looked round – no one. I took a step in the direction of the hotel and heard a heart-rending cry literally beneath my feet. I looked down and saw two Lilliputians, one of whom was writhing in pain. It was a man; he was hopping on one leg, holding the other in his hands. Beside him stood a female Lilliputian, trying to calm him as best she could. I guessed that the non-meeting of the day before had been initiated by them and I was impatient to convince myself of this and also to know who they were and what had brought them to me. Sensing that the conversation would be lengthy, I decided to invite them to my room, especially as the dreary autumn weather did not incline one to chat at all. They cheerfully agreed, as if they had been expecting this invitation.

The hotel administrator regarded my companions with surprise but, without saying anything, handed me the keys to my room. I regaled my guests with coffee and we regarded one another in silence and total bemusement. The injured party broke the silence. He stood up from the armchair – he would have been better not to do that – I at once lost him from view, but, as if nothing had happened, he dived out from under the coffee table and introduced himself theatrically: "Voldemar." Pointing to the armchair where his companion was sitting, he said, with the same intonation: "My spouse, Magdalena." He added, with special pride: "A merited artiste of the Soviet Union." I continued to sit in silence not knowing how to react and how to get on to the subject of what had been agitating me for the last twenty-four hours.

In order to fill the pause which again arose, I began to scrutinize Magdalena. She sensed I was looking at her, but, in no way flustered, behaved calmly and fairly independently. In her dress with its stiff collar she resembled Thumbelina. It seemed to me that one more second and she would begin to spin on her axis. My thoughts were interrupted by the voice of Magdalena, childish, piercing and setting my teeth on edge. For the first few minutes I did not even try to understand what she was talking about. My sole wish was to get out of the room, but the unexpectedness of it made me cover my ears with my hands; I did not know what would come next. Magdalena immediately came up to me and with her gentle little hands tore my hands away from my ears and, looking me in the eye, said maternally: "Excuse me, please. Excitement caused that. Now I will speak quietly and in no circumstances will I occasion you any moments of unpleasantness." I calmed down and realised that there were no more threats to me.

Suddenly it seemed to me that I had seen this pair somewhere else. Straining my memory and not holding back my emotions, I literally yelled: "Wait! How can this be? Can it really be you?" My new acquaintances, not knowing what else to expect from me, tried to leave. But I cut off their retreat, picked them up in turn and seated them in armchairs, like babies in a pram. Voldemar's look of jealousy when I picked up Magdalena, did not escape me.

Once again silence reigned in the room. Fantastic! How could I have forgotten them? After all, Voldemar and Magdalena lived in my yard and it was precisely the image of

Voldemar which had appeared to me before my trip and asked whether I'd not been in Odesa for a long time. I immediately shared my discoveries with my guests, and my guesses did not evoke any surprise in them. Voldemar intriguingly said: "It was all like that," adding: "With your recollections you've fulfilled our mission." He again slipped out of the armchair, emerged from under the coffee table and bowed several times, as if he were standing in a circus ring and gratefully accepting the audience's applause.

I needed to begin a conversation, but something was stopping me. Finally I realised what it was that was giving me no rest. I immediately turned to Voldemar: "How has this come about? Since our last meeting on the Moldavanka, more than fifty years have passed, but you haven't changed or, if you'll forgive my saying so, aged. This is more like a circus trick than real life. Who are you in reality? And how old are you? Maybe it's not you at all, but your doubles?" As I posed these questions, I paid close attention to the expressions on their faces. Not a muscle or a nerve so much as twitched, nothing at any rate outwardly, expressed either unease or wariness.

My opponents, and above all Voldemar, who crossed his arms on his chest and frowned a little, waited for the end of my monologue, and as soon as that happened, he said calmly, even cold-bloodedly: "You mustn't be upset or nervous. We are us and we really did live in the same yard as you more than fifty years ago. The only thing we earnestly entreat you is this: don't be surprised at anything and believe our every word and then everything will be all right with us." At that point I could restrain myself no longer and tried to reply sharply: "Be so good as to tell me, what should happen? All the same, how old are you?" Raising his voice, but, at the same time, calmly, as if straining the words through his teeth, said: "My friend, you see we really don't know how old we are, we're from another reality."

After hearing this, I felt I was going mad. It suddenly seemed to me that there was no one in the room and that I was talking to myself. In order to convince myself of the opposite, I stood up abruptly, which again probably frightened my guests, went up to them and squatted down in front of the armchairs, so that I felt their excited breath on me. Convinced that they were real and not the fruit of my hallucinations, I returned to my place and said: "All right, no more about age. But, if it's not a secret, what does your mission consist of, the mission you have spoken about so persuasively from the moment we met?"

Voldemar sighed with relief, wiped the sweat from his brow with a black silk handkerchief and again, as he had done at the beginning of our conversation, said intriguingly: "To prepare you for the most important meeting of your life."

After what I'd heard, I noticed that objects in the room had started to move. The chandelier on the ceiling began to rotate on its axis as if in the big top circus motorcyclists were rushing at great speed over the wooden planking. Magdalena unexpectedly joined in our dialogue. As she had promised, she spoke in a whisper, as softly and trustingly as possible: "Don't be afraid. I understand you. It's difficult for you to believe what Voldemar said. But it's the honest truth – we really don't know our age. And we came to see you involuntarily, in order to prepare you for the upcoming meeting. Tell me, how would we have met you here if you had not remembered about your vision? I hope you've worked out now why Voldemar's question about whether you had been in Odesa for a long time was not a chance question. And the fact that you've appeared here and that we were neighbours – are those not links in a chain of events preordained by those who have power over us and for whom time is no more than clay in the hands of a potter." Magdalena's words flew about the room like multi-coloured butterflies, settling on my shoulders, my wrists and even my eyelashes.

For a moment I felt I had shrunk to the size of a cigarette lighter. Voldemar and Magdalena now seemed huge to me. Now Voldemar, hands behind his back began to strut round the room importantly, like a peacock. I realised that any minute they would see what had happened to me, so I crawled down from the armchair and tried to hide unobtrusively in the corner, behind a standard lamp. I was almost halfway there when I noticed that Voldemar was advancing on me. If it had not been for Magdalena's soul-searing cry, Voldemar would have crushed me. His foot was literally hanging over my head. Voldemar froze, looking at me as if I were a small insect, took me by the scruff of the neck, lifted me up to his face, began to examine me with extreme contempt and, seeing nothing of interest, squeamishly threw me onto Magdalena's knees.

After the horror I'd been through, I finally felt safe. For the first time I became aware how defenceless mankind is in this world, but the most surprising thing was that Voldemar had somehow read my thoughts and continued aloud: "… if mankind does not have faith." So saying, he again took me in his massive mitt and carefully placed me in the armchair, where, in a matter of seconds, my body resumed its former shape. As soon as this happened, the first thing I did was to hurry up to the mirror and, not believing my eyes, to examine myself, first with my left hand and then with my right hand. Watching me attentively my guests, for the first time since our meeting, did not simply smile – there was unvarnished warmth in their looks.

Voldemar was the first to break the silence, saying, in a good-natured tone: "We've stayed here for a good long time. If anything was wrong, we're sorry." I, overcome with emotion, literally blurted out: "Come off it! It was all so un-expected and surprising." "That's excellent," said Voldemar, after which he and Magdalena headed for the door, and I didn't try to stop them.

Voldemar was already in the doorway when he, appar-ently by chance, struck his forehead with his hand and said confidingly, as if someone might hear him: "I almost forgot to say the most important thing. You've no objection to meeting an envoy tomorrow?" It was then I recalled the be-ginning of our confused conversation. I clearly understood that there was no sense in refusing, since nothing depended on my decision, but Voldemar added: "What do you mean? Something definitely depends on it. Your goodwill is needed for everything." Whereupon, without further thought, I said: "Of course, I agree." "That's terrific," said Voldemar. "So, till tomorrow." "Forgive me," – the words burst from my lips – "but how…" "I'll ring you." "But you don't know my phone number." In reply Voldemar merely smiled and he and Magdalena, like little hedgehogs, rolled out of the room. As soon as the door closed behind them, I fell asleep in a weakened state.

The ring of my mobile phone woke me. I heard Volde-mar's voice: "We weren't going to disturb you while you were asleep. If you've no objection let's meet at eleven o'clock at the same spot as before." I replied: "Of course I've no objection." But no one heard me – the phone again went dead.

It was dark outside the window. Had my sleep really lasted less than an hour? To my surprise the hands of my watch showed it was just after eight. There were less than two hours to go before our meeting. I was in a state of total prostration. It couldn't be said that I did not want to think about the upcoming meeting – I simply could not think, insofar as I was devastated and bereft of strength. At first, I decided to resort to alcohol, but at once thought better of it and decided to go for a stroll in the fresh air, in the hope that this would buck me up, but I sensed that this would clearly be insufficient. Unfortunately, my imagination, by dint of a series of circumstances, refused to seek an exit from a most complex situation.

I quickly got dressed and went out onto Primorsky Boulevard. A penetrating wind off the sea twirled my bones like prayer-beads. But this did not last long. I just had to turn the corner for the wind to drop; there was moisture in the air and a state of physical exhaustion took hold of me with even greater force. When my despair reached its apogee, I heard a voice. I felt that someone with a very pleasant timbre was addressing me from invisible celestial spheres: "Don't despair. Everything will soon pass and you will be full of strength and energy, as in your youth."

Indeed, in a couple of minutes I became another man; it seemed that one more step, and I would take off. I don't know from where the strength came, and not only strength – every muscle was in play and summoned me to action. When I clenched my fist, the crunching of the air could be heard. I realised that this could not be, but it was. Now I was ready for the meeting.

Suddenly the realisation struck me that there was no need to look at my watch. That meant that if I stood in the appointed place and time stood still alongside me and, on his watch – it's eleven in the evening. Thus it was in actual fact. A few minutes later Voldemar and Magdalena came up to me. Now there were four of us waiting for the upcoming meeting – me, time and my two new friends.

The street was deserted and I could discern someone of just over medium height approaching us unhurriedly and with a confident gait. I had no doubt that he was precisely the person whose acquaintance I was about to make imminently. He came up, gave me his hand and introduced himself – "Levitsky."

Before me stood a nondescript man but for his eyes, which were a heavenly colour. As soon as I looked into them, inexplicable things began to happen to me. First, a chill ran through me, then I became feverish and I felt I was losing consciousness. I instantly averted my gaze and at once regained my former equilibrium. "You said Levitsky?" "Yes, my name is Levitsky." "A remarkable coincidence. I knew a Levitsky. He was a childhood friend. We went to school together – we were in the same class. A few days before the final exams, to the surprise of all of us, he disappeared. Strange as it may seem, his disappearance was most deeply felt by my grandmother. Forgive me, this story does not, of course, concern you at all, and, what's more, your age tells me that the events which I've just recalled happened long before you were born." "But no, my friend. I am that self-same Levitsky," the man replied with a faint smile. At that point I could not restrain myself: "You're joking. I wasn't born yesterday. If you'd seen even once what the real Levitsky looked like you wouldn't indulge in such inappropriate jokes. I don't know you, and I don't want to."

He began to apologise. "I didn't want to offend you in any way. I got it wrong. I should have set up our conversation differently. But don't upset yourself. It's not too late to correct things." "I don't know what you want to correct, but for the last two days I've exhausted myself so much that I wasn't up for jokes, especially not jokes from a stranger." "You're right. But all the same I ask you not to go away. I've really got a lot to tell you. Only please, don't interrupt me, at least for the first ten minutes. Agreed? Then let's begin."

"Firstly, for you, Shurik (that's what I think your close friends called you, as did Grandmother Fanya, whom we both loved), I am that same clumsy Kolya Levitsky, with the wall left eye." After he spoke these words, I felt I had sunk up to my waist into the ground, but he went on: "I know what you're thinking about now. You don't believe me and, in your eyes, I appear as a chancer, since you don't rule out the possibility that one of my friends could have told me this story. Even if this is so, I nevertheless advise you to be patient and to find out why I've brought you to this meeting with me. That wasn't a slip of the tongue: it was really me that brought you. I won't rehearse everything that preceded our meeting; I'll merely say that my assistants Voldemar and Magdalena played a not insignificant role in this. But let's not get distracted by detail. I hope you haven't forgotten how the three of us – you, Senya Yukhtman and I used to steal peaches in the Michurinsky Gardens and hide them in our shirt fronts. Only for some reason, unlike the two of you, I got no irritation on my body and my peaches, if you remember, ripened, while yours rotted. And what about the games we played together – Cossacks, bandits, *mayalka…*

And in order to remove completely your doubts regarding my identity, I'll remind you of just one episode from our schooldays. When you asked me why I didn't study, I hope you've forgotten what I said in reply: 'But why should I? I know everything anyway.' And finally, those unforgettable dinners at your grandmother's and my reluctance, after the meal, to utter the simple human word 'thanks' was not fortuitous – I simply wanted to convince myself that Grandma Fanya was doing good, because she had a pure soul, and her soul required nothing in exchange. But, following me with her eyes, almost in a whisper, as if trying to take a load off my heart, she would say *akhmunes* – I'm sorry for the child. So then, shall I go on?" "No, don't."

I was pitiful to look at. I realised it was pointless to enquire how, instead of a left wall eye, a perfectly healthy eye had appeared, or why he looked so young that I found it difficult to come to terms with the fact that he was my age.

Levitsky began to talk again. "Incidentally, I didn't disappear then. It was simply that my mission was complete and I had to return."

Naturally, I didn't ask what mission he was talking about or where Levitsky had to return to. I was now convinced that this really was Levitsky and proposed that we started using the familiar form of address. Levitsky concurred.

"The story of my appearance on the Moldavanka was not a matter of chance. In this world in general nothing is, or ever can be, a matter of chance. So then, we will first mention your great grandfather, Shlomo, the father of your Grandma Fanya. At that time they lived in a village near Korosten. But Shlomo was not simply a Hasidic, not simply a Rebbe, he was already a real, but hidden righteous man. And after his death his soul occupied an honoured place in the Garden of Eden, that is in Paradise. Where his soul was, even we angels cannot be. His merits were so great before the Creator that I was charged not only with protecting Grandma Fanya, whom he called Frumka and whom, after the Almighty, of course, he loved more than anything in the world, but also with protecting all the remaining close relatives, to the third generation, in order to amend and improve their earthly passage, especially yours. So, I appeared in Odesa."

"But how did you protect me, if that's not a secret?" I asked with interest. "Firstly, I spent most of my time with you. Secondly, I protected you several times from wounds and mutilations and even saved you from death. Is it possible you don't remember? Although it's not surprising – children are the biggest egoists in the world; they notice no one apart from themselves. You loved to hang on to the special handrails. In Odesa that's called 'riding the bumper.' On one such journey, when the tram unexpectedly braked sharply, to avoid knocking down a drunk pedestrian, you lost your balance and were thrown off. I literally caught you in flight. You were in such a state then that this episode did not stay in your memory. But do you remember how you and I swam to the buoy on Arcadia Beach? Some youths swam up and tried to drown you… I could adduce still more examples but I think you're convinced of the accuracy of my words."

I nodded submissively and Levitsky went on with his story. "The life of Grandma Fanya was much more interesting. During the war she was left without a husband and, with four children on her hands, had no means of support. There were days when there wasn't a crumb of bread on the table. The children and Grandma herself could have starved to death. Then I brought a Singer sewing machine and left it in the attic. Beside it I put two sacks; one was stuffed with black material and threads, the other with cotton wool. Then I arranged for your grandmother to go up into the attic and find all this by chance. Thus she began to make soft warm *valenki* boots and sell them in the bazaar. That saved her and the children. Then your mother's younger brother discovered a talent for drawing. And again, Grandma Fanya found canvas and paints in the attic. Your Uncle Dima, a boy of seven, painted a portrait of Stalin; your grandmother sold it for what was, at the time, a large sum and the family survived until Victory day. Thus the soul of Shloma protected you."

I was crushed. Grandma Fanya had told me many times how she made *valenki* to sell and how Uncle Dima had done a portrait of Stalin. With every minute that passed I was gripped by fear and trembling. I could not believe what was happening, but before me stood someone who called himself Levitsky and had, in a matter of minutes, related not only my life, but the life of my grandmother and her children.

Now I realised that this was the prelude to the main conversation. I looked down at Voldemar and Magdalena who were standing there dumbfounded and in total silence. Their faces expressed obedience and reverence, and this was clearly not fear, but something bigger, something akin to when we look at the moon or sun, realising that they are not simply beyond our consciousness, but something un-attainable, without which our lives not only have no sense, but simply do not exist.

Standing before Levitsky, I became aware of the lack of correlation between what we are, what we feel, and spiritual reality. Once again, as in the hotel room, I felt myself to be a bug, a speck of dust, but a moment later I seemed to be recharged, like a battery, and that charge of energy, with which an otherworldly power had endowed me, was melting away before my eyes. This meeting was like an earthquake; I had the feeling I had fallen into a dreadful abyss from which it was impossible to escape. I lacked air and was gasping for breath.

Summoning up the last of my strength I looked at my watch; the hands stood like sentries and showed eleven o'clock. After a prolonged pause, Levitsky uttered just two words: "t'shuvah" and "tikkun" – repentance and rectitude.

Without saying goodbye, I set off for the hotel and once in my room, without undressing, I fell asleep. A deafening knock on the door woke me up. Half asleep, I opened it and saw before me a whole delegation of hotel staff, headed by the director who, not holding back his emotions, asked: "What's happened to you? You haven't left your room for three days. We didn't know what to think. If you hadn't opened the door just now, we'd have been forced to break it down. It's good that everything's OK!" I did not begin to justify myself or apologise; there was no sense in doing so.

When the guests left the room, I turned my attention to the unusual envelope on the coffee table. I remember exactly that when I had returned the day before, it hadn't been there. I opened the envelope and saw a plane ticket with today's date and the flight time – 13.00 hours. Outside the window it was morning, my watch showed just after ten. I quickly got my things together, hailed a taxi and, on the way to the airport, on one of the pedestrian crossings, saw two Lilliputians, resembling Voldemar and Magdalena. They were crossing the street unhurriedly. It even seemed to me that Voldemar turned his head towards me and, smiling slyly, winked.

KUNA

Where do you think that unique anthropological brood, namely the Kuna family, might live, the brood whom you are in line to meet, or, to be more precise, where could it not live? Of course, anywhere except Odesa.

In Odesa no one believes in anything, but everyone trusts one another. People are one thing but Odesites are quite another. Not only do they want to live beautifully, they do live beautifully. Not all of them, admittedly, but that's another story.

Odesa, like any well-born lady, has immunity from bandits, from talented musicians, from *wunderkinder* and illicit dealers, from academics and sailors, from writers and Jews.

Odesites are people with a mind of their own; from childhood they despise public transport, and if they are called to the city, they cannot do without taxis. Well, just tell me who is going to respect you if you come out of a tram or a bus. Only people like you but for the Odesite it means nothing. You want to excite yourself and talk about elevated things, about the meaning of life. All right. Go ahead. Why not? The whole meaning of life for an Odesite is to eat well. What else is left in life when there is nothing left. What about talking?

In our city conversation always goes along a sloping surface; in dialogue the most important thing is not to slip into the ungrateful channel of negative emotions. Conversation must flow smoothly, unhurriedly, transitioning to elevated tones. How else can colour be added to a conversation, how can one insult someone to their face, and in such a way that they think nothing of it, and the lucky fellow is cut to the quick; that. I tell you, is not childish flim-flam but serious science. And may you be spared praising someone; the conversation then turns into a pitiful facsimile of a eulogy and your interlocutor turns into a wrinkled apple or, even worse, into a freeze-dried herbarium.

In talking about Odesa, it is impossible not to recall its tourist sights, the sea and the Potemkin Steps about the Duc[15] and, of course, about the children. Children in Odesa are a caste of untouchables; people do not only love them, they rejoice in them, and if a child is insufficiently well-fed, or slightly undernourished, that means it's not an Odesa child.

Our story has come smoothly to its beginning and if you ask what happened before, that does not mean anything to me; perhaps someone has simply guided my hand over the paper, or else the words have come themselves, like a herd of sheep to the pasture of a blank sheet; there they graze and fill the pasture with meaning.

Odesites always have a choice. And if you ask me what that is, I will reply without thinking: how do I know? And so, *bikitser* – quick sticks! In the sixties, if you had money and your nerves were shot, you could escape from your beloved neighbours in the communal flat either to the cemetery or

....

[15]   Duc of Richelieu, Odesa's town governor between 1803 and 1814. At the top of the stairs is the Duc de Richelieu Monument, unveiled in 1826.

to the cooperative apartment block in Cheryomushki. Kuna and Nyuma could allow themselves this, and did so, buying a cooperative flat; that is, they chose the dessert over the first course and who, as they say could gainsay them?

Nyuma was not an underground – and illegal – workshop owner. These were the same revolutionaries who, like bricklayers built the foundations of capitalism in the bowels of socialism. Nyuma was simply the head of a workshop in a varnish and paint factory. As you can imagine, paint and varnish are the sort of chemical substances that people have quite enough of, so long as they have their health. The Odesite who can't make his *parnusa*, his livelihood, is nailed for life to the column of shame of public opinion. In Odesa no one will ever give away a *asheine meidede* – a beauty from a good family – to a *mishiginer*, a mad engineer, *of gantse kop*, who's right off his head. Let it not be said of us, thought Nyuma, and he would be right, for the moment forgetting that their son Misha, the elder brother of Gavrik, was just such a source of *tsuris,* of trouble.

You won't believe this, but Nyuma was a quiet, unconfident man; no one in his family was overly fond of him, beginning with Kuna and ending with the cat. He was ashamed of himself, considered himself a burden and, unlike Kuna or Gavrik and Misha was unable to do nothing for days on end, as they were. So it was that at the crack of dawn, filled with embarrassment, scarcely breathing, he tiptoed out of his flat, put on his shoes in the doorway and set off to work. At the paint and varnish factory he was to be reckoned with, but that was small consolation for him. He felt drawn to Kuna, but Kuna was drawn in the opposite direction, and so they lived, cheek by jowl.

Kuna was, above all, a sister, mother and wife, purely by compulsion. Kuna hid her aristocratic origins beneath the ruins of domesticity and felt herself to be a defenceless Thumbelina surrounded by three uncouth blockheads. Her refined nature dreamed of other things; sometimes her timid soul gave her away, but with each year that passed there were fewer and fewer such betrayals, like echoes – now an abstracted gaze into the distance, from one room to another, now a deep guttural sigh – as if someone were trying to throttle her and with the last of her strength she took in air in greedy gulps, and was overcome by an asthmatic cough; but by an effort of will Kuna broke free of the iron fetters and strolled about the flat as if nothing was amiss. Scarcely anyone who knew her could imagine Kuna hurrying to work. Her external appearance alone was reminiscent of some Biblical character lost in an untidy urban flat. It was as if time had played a dirty trick on Kuna by transporting her several centuries into the future. But what is the point of complaining about Fate when you can't change anything anyway.

The sum total of Kuna was some skirts, aprons, blouses, headscarves and other bits and pieces which bore no relation to life beyond her flat. You got the impression that all grease stains had made their exodus from the kitchen and found their long-awaited promised rest on her intricate get-up. Kuna reminded you of a sacrificial animal. It seemed that a minute more and the lot would fall on her and the Chief Priest would send her to the wilderness of Azazel and throw her off a cliff, and only then would begin the service for Yom Kippur.

Kuna did not speak; she mumbled, keened, whispered, sighed, gulped and asked to be left in peace.

It was long past midnight. Kuna was sitting in an armchair in front of a television which had been switched on, and was dozing helplessly. Her glasses in their black frames hung precariously on her nose. It seemed that if a movie hero had raised his voice, it would definitely have disrupted their balance and they would not simply have fallen but would have crashed down with all the weight of the day's sights and experiences onto the magazine lying on Kuna's lap. How the magazine had turned up there was difficult to say, but it was reliably known that Kuna never read. Kuna and reading were obviously mutually exclusive concepts, but, obviously, such was the will of Providence.

When Gavrik, like a housebreaker, tried to open the door quietly and enter the flat, Kuna immediately woke up and, in spite of the late hour, rushed into action. Before her stood a perplexed Gavrik, his arms spread wide. Unlike Kuna, for him this seemed more than adequate. Without pausing for thought, Kuna opened the door to Misha's room; he, as usual, was sitting there in his underpants, listening to music.

"Just look at that layabout! The milk isn't dry on his lips, but already he's like a mating tom cat in March, having a high old time."

Gavrik's lips moved soundlessly.

"Ma-ma," said Misha lackadaisically.

"What do you mean by that? You'd do better to look at your brother," she said, turning towards Gavrik. "Do you think I don't know what you're doing with Svetka from the first floor, you idle so-and-so, and she's old enough to be your mother."

"So what?" replied Misha, again lazily.

Misha was not overfond of Gavrik; Gavril did not like working, and in this they were in agreement. Kuna also did not like working and, what's more, she didn't like Nyuma, but he was the breadwinner. Kuna could not understand how he managed this, given his brains, but she persuaded herself not to think about this. After all, she could think about things about which Nyuma would never allow himself to think.

But we're not talking about Kuna, but Misha. He always answered any question with a question. There were various questions, but only one answer: "But why?" He never got to the end of a sentence – he couldn't be bothered to do so. Misha liked frilly phrases or, to be more precise, feral phrases, like the fringe of a plush tablecloth. His sentences broke off, congealed, like breadcrumbs, into little balls and he would chuck them into the faces of either Kuna or Gavrik. Misha dreamed of living apart. The dream quietly mocked him, whether from desperation or because Misha and she had to share one roof. She too wanted to live apart from Misha.

We've diverted from our narrative by paying tribute to Misha, but it's time to return to our heroine.

Kuna was not calming down.

"No, just look. Svetka is well over forty, while my *nakhes*, the apple of my eye, is well under twenty. While she said this, she poked Gavrik insistently in the chest with her index finger.

On that note, the nightly exchange of fire, as usual, fizzled out and everyone began to get ready for bed peacefully.

Kuna's dream was militantly alarming. She pictured Svetka in such unsightly poses that cold sweat began to run down the back of her neck and make its way into the depths of Kuna's inflamed consciousness. "Something must be done with that bitch." After these words a bitter hoar frost of contempt appeared on Kuna's lips, which were parched with disgust. "I'll sort her out tomorrow." After such a decisive conclusion she felt better, curled herself up in a ball like a small child and gave herself up to pleasant dreams.

The morning turned out gloomy, heralding nothing good for Svetka. An encounter took place completely by chance at the door of Svetka's flat, where Kuna had been standing on guard since six o'clock in the morning. Breathing heavily, and constantly tidying a stray lock of grey hair, Kuna said in a quiet voice, but in such a way that it was audible not only in the entrance lobby but also in the street:

"Svetka, that's not on!"

To which Svetka, in no way embarrassed, replied:

"So what is on?"

At these words Kuna was not only taken aback, but somehow subsided, somehow shrank. Her eyebrows straightened and stood one above the other, rather like the narrow tramway along which the toy Belgian trams of the NEP era ran down Frunze Street, from Moldavanka to Peresyp. Svetka now took Kuna delicately by her heaving shoulders and said in a kindly voice:

"Citizeness, move aside. It's time for me to go out on business."

Kuna lurched to one side like a sleepwalker, and Svetka disappeared in the sunlight, which had burst into the lobby like an uninvited guest.

"What a bitch!" said Kuna in a tremulous tone, recovering her composure.

The incident was concluded. Kuna was defeated, the gladiatorial contest was over before it began. It only remained for Kuna to await the verdict of a crowd of infuriated emotions. Kuna was returning home via a stairwell where every step brought her closer to Golgotha. Gavrik and Misha were waiting for her at home. Kuna had one last chance to restore her spiritual equilibrium and that chance was called: "really rubbing Gavrik's nose in it." An anxious Gavrik met her.

"Mama, where did you get to so early?"

"Right," said Kuna's inner voice, "the gauntlet is thrown down." Kuna took two steps towards Gavrik and shoved her head under his chin.

"Look me straight in the eyes," Kuna hissed, adding: "You and Svetka resemble one another as Dyukovsky Park[16] does the Champs-Élysées with rice."

At this point Misha could no longer restrain himself.

"Mama, what fields? What rice?"

Kuna dealt him a swinging blow.

"Misha, you're as clever as your Jupiter tape recorder."

Gavrik tried to take advantage of the lull to escape from the flat. No such luck. As a true Marxist, Kuna did not allow her opponent to collect himself.

"No, just look at those urchins," Kuna called out to a space entirely devoid of hooligans. "Misha, please don't brew my brains. I'm not that Ceylon tea of yours. Do you like that, Hercules? For once in your life you might put something on that skeleton besides pants. Oh, I was forgetting. You're a crudist."

"Mama," countered Misha, "not a crudist – a nudist."

"Maybe, so what does that change? I have to sort out this rubbish – this *tukhes*[17] – from early morning. If only Nyuma hadn't been at work, although what does that change?

....

[16]   This is one of the oldest parks in Odesa, laid out in 1810 by the order of Duc de Richelieu near his country residence.

[17]   Literally means "one's bottom."

Although this evening I'll give him valerian drops from my tears. That may help."

"Who?" said Misha with interest.

"Your papa, of course, and at last he'll take an interest in you. But all the same, I'll grab her by her ginger hair and drag her all round the yard. Let all the neighbours see how she found love at first shite."

"Mama, not shite. Sight," said Misha, carefully correcting her.

"Misha, if you speak to me again as I've asked you not to, I'll cause you such an *azohen vey* that I won't need to do anything more."

The day was approaching its end with intermittent success and Nyuma appeared unexpectedly in the doorway. He always appeared unexpectedly – after all, no one expected him. He quickly assessed the situation and tried to slip in quietly, but no such luck. He would have tasted his share of Kuna's anger if Mirra, Kuna's sister, the meekest being on earth, had not appeared behind him.

"That'll do. Shush!" whispered Kuna ingratiatingly and, without uttering another word, set off, as usual, for the kitchen, to cook and serve supper.

Mirra was an old maid and taught mathematics to senior classes, but this had been of no help to Gavrik in his time. She lived almost in the centre of the city, on Ostrovidova Street, in a communal flat, where a female teacher of maths could still live.

After supper everyone dispersed to their rooms, but Kuna remained with Mirra in the kitchen, and the conversation began with "*Vus erzakh?*" – How's things? As always, Mirra shrugged her shoulders timidly and, without waiting for an answer, Kuna began to rail against Fate.

Mirra knew Kuna's revelations by heart, down to the last comma, and never interrupted, understanding that her sister needed to have her say. And who but her would listen to these *piste manses*, these vacuous stories? As a rule Kuna would end her monologue with the words "I'll drop in tomorrow." That meant that the next day Kuna would bring Mirra the next instalment of money, honestly earned by Nyuma, and, together with it, some gold and jewellery.

Mirra once asked her elder sister "Why do you keep all this stuff at my place?" "Where else could I keep it? I've only got one sister. As you realise, I can't keep it at home. You've got a communal flat. Who would think of looking there? The Department against Misappropriation isn't interested in you. Why should they look for stuff in other people's flats? They've got enough of their own. But people like Nyuma are always in their sights. So hide it and don't ask stupid questions." And Mirra didn't.

Kuna had a nervous attitude to money and at night she would count it carefully and would examine every banknote through a magnifying glass, taking a strong dislike to old state-issue notes. But in the morning, she would thrust Nyuma's nose into the banknotes and, taking pity on him, give him a small sum for lunch in the factory canteen.

So ran the life of this middle-income Odesa family. Kuna was always concerned with domestic issues while Nyuma engaged in subversive activity against the Soviet economy and toiled way for token money; Gavrik pursued Svetka; Misha listened to the Beatles or Led Zeppelin and berated Kuna. It seemed as if this would go on forever.

But one fine day Nyuma was no more. He died at night, as quietly as he had lived, without saying a word. "A good death," said Kuna, and burst into tears.

But that money, oh, that money. When it's there we don't notice in it; when it runs out, we begin to hate it, but not so much as to do without it.

At first Kuna sold her gold, then she sold her diamonds, but neither Gavrik nor Misha decided to start working for a living. "Too late for me," Misha would say, "and what will you get out of Gavrik?" Indeed, there was nothing to be got out of him. Mirra remained the sole breadwinner. She moved in with Kuna, but what's the point of a maths teacher? "Something must be done," said Kuna, gazing into Misha's eyes, which promised nothing. Misha, Socrates-like, proclaimed: "You must blame me."

Once again life, as before, began to revolve and display new colours. Misha was the first to go out into the street. He and Gavrik disappeared somewhere for days on end, made arrangements about something by phone, and illegal samizdat literature appeared in the flat. So they became real anti-Soviet activists. The brothers fervently loathed Soviet power and Kuna served as a visual aid for them. Time brought them remorselessly ever nearer the OVIR visa office.

With Nyuma's demise, Kuna was plunged into a balloon-like void. With every passing minute the balloon was filled with her breath, the earth began to give way under her feet and the balloon began to gain height. Lightning flashed above her head, thunder rolled, and from the depths of non-existence a familiar voice resounded. "Kuna, where are you going?" "He's still asking! To you, of course." "No, Kuna, that wasn't yet the arrangement," said Nyuma in a quiet, ingratiating voice. "You need to be with the children, with our boys." "I won't go back." "Kuna, you're again looking out for yourself. Just listen to me for once and don't argue."

And, for the first time, Kuna did not argue.

NYUSYA

It's a strange feeling – whether autumn excites and cools the blood of recollections like tinted glass, or whether speechlessness, burrowing into the haystack of silence, conveys to everyone around your class-bases hatred for what is happening, with which you, as defined by your own soul, wish to have no truck. However, what significance this does have in the tunnel of blunted feelings, in the unconscious dead-end of the geographical place where you turned up, not by the whim of fate, but by pure chance, having come across a notice beneath the roof of the mass consciousness of your fellow tribespeople.

"Everyone is leaving. It's time for us to go," said Fima to Nyusya and, like everyone else, they went in any direction they could: some went to Germany, which had unexpectedly taken a liking to Jews, but our heroes obtained permanent residency in Israel. And so there I was, strolling down the promenade in Tel Aviv, along the Mediterranean.

Nyusya, have you been scared by something? What do you mean? This is the only place where solitude and my memories make me happy. Pay no attention to my wary look. How could it be otherwise – after all, I'm gazing fixedly into the past. Solitude is my sole privilege after relocating. But do you know what's surprising? Memories are not behind me; they precede me and lay down a path, distancing me from the present. I have the feeling that one more step and I, like Alice, will be through the looking glass and Odesa will begin. And how did this all begin? Why, as it does with everyone. I don't remember the details. The associations of what I've lived through don't leave me, like a shadow which holds you on the leash of time in the eventide of a dying day. Do you remember that scene from the Antonioni film? I see a big white ship sailing down the streets of Odesa, picking up all those who wish to leave their unforgettable native land. What was that like? A civil war, the arrival of the Reds, only we weren't fleeing from the Revolution but from ourselves. Did everyone think that? Get away with you! No one thought about anything at all. Those leaving infected those who still hesitated; the air itched with impatience and it seemed that in a day or two it would burst like a soap bubble and life would cease to exist in the present. Only the future would remain, like a tram crammed to the gunwales – you have to manage to jump onto its platform, otherwise you'll remain in the past. And what about the white ship? What news of it? It crossed the equator between Moldavanka and Peresyp and has concealed itself in neutral waters. And did that serve as the point of no return for you? There were the empty shop counters of the nineties and the miserable, joyless faces of the passers-by. It seemed that life had lost its colour, had faded. The sea reminded one of an ordinary puddle in front of an apartment block; there were no ships, not even any pleasure boats. Your eyes refused to believe in what was happening. Yes, even then Odesa lived by its own laws, but that did not save you from discomfort or depression. Only those who did not know a better life could endure. It was terrifying to contemplate Odesa. Furthermore, Fima had taken it into his head to go to Israel on a tourist visa. He came back a changed man. The contrast was such that he didn't speak, but roared, like an enraged beast. Everything was decided in no time. But how was life for you in Odesa? After all, you're from Balta, from the province where neither time nor changes in ourselves have any power.

So there I was, walking along a dusty lane with mama, my hand stuck like plantain to her warm hand. Two snow-white ribbons floated above my lop-sided pigtails – celestial tokens of childish happiness. A vast square opened up before us – Bazaar Square, the triumph of our life. Mother increased her pace, the scenes changed, as if I were travelling by tram and looking enquiringly out of the window. Mother had two chickens in a string bag. The mesh of the net was digging in to their inert bodies and their feathers were sticking through, as if they were waving white flags and begging for mercy. My heart was breaking and awash with blood, like the combs of the doomed chickens. If only our ancestors had not sinned and there had been no flood, if only God had not allowed Noah and, by extension, all of us, to use the meat of animals as food. But there was no way back. We were going to the *shochet* and he, according to Jewish tradition, was to behead the hapless chickens and return them to us plucked. In that fashion and in no other fashion. We would have kosher soup on the table, with boiled chicken, boiled potatoes and onions, and cabbage which mother had salted in oaken casks. Lovely grub! But how could I overcome the pity within me? I walked along, crying. My mother pretended not to notice my tears, but I can tell what is in her heart. The residence of the *shochet* is like a dilapidated wooden barn which would have collapsed long ago had it not been propped up by the bazaar fence. Inside the residence were mountains of chicken feathers, like slag heaps, only white. As soon as you crossed the threshold of this crematorium, an incredibly dreadful smell induced a state of semi-consciousness; having passed through a nauseating fog, you approached within touching distance of the *shochet* and handed over for slaughter the beloved chickens with whom you used to play in the courtyard. Waves of sickly, sticky air propelled you out into the fresh air, like a cork from a champagne bottle. Meanwhile, mountains of feathers fly upwards like angels, begging for mercy. I waited for mother by the door. Ten minutes later she appeared with the slaughtered and plucked chickens. I regarded her with loathing and, unable to restrain myself, accused her of murder. Mother contemplated me in silence with a vacant, other-worldly stare and, without saying anything, took me by the hand and we went home like two people alienated from one another. In the middle of the familiar lane mother inexplicably halted and, looking over me into the distance, said (it was not clear to whom), "Forgive me." We set off again as a couple and forgot what had happened between us. Thus are born secrets.

But where are you? To whom am I telling this? I'm right here. Why have you attached yourself to me? Why are you tormenting my soul? It is in enough pain as it is. Although, to tell the truth, I'm pleased with you. Why do you say nothing about yourself, but merely ask questions and I, like an idiot, do nothing else but answer. But maybe that's even better. Why should I know about you? In actual fact, Nyusya, everything is completely the other way round. You ask, and I answer in your voice. So, you turn out to be a mystic? What do you mean? I'm an ordinary spirit, the mirror image of your soul. Your breath is my will too, or to be precise, yours; it wanders like an echo through the labyrinth of your veins and you bring it forth into the light. I sense it, I see it with my spiritual vision. A little more and I'll begin to fear not you, but myself. After all, there's no one beside me.

I know you miss Odesa. Miss it very much. I was there a couple of years ago. Really? Yes. How was it? Don't ask. I barely stuck it for a day and the next day I took off. Everything was alien and everyone thought me an alien. Where are you now? Nowhere. Not here, not there. I'm somewhere between heaven and earth. I'm a pendulum of recollections. I oscillate between past life and present life. Surprisingly, after I returned from Odesa, Israel became a closer and more kindred place for me, but my yearning for Odesa merely increased. But what about Fima? He's in good heart. Actually, he misses it much more than I do. There he felt at home, in his element, but here we're *Aliyah*, migrants. In Odesa we were often called yids, but here we're Russians. You must understand, my friend, where our motherland is. Fima constantly finds pretexts for flying off to Odesa, to his sister while she was alive, now to his niece and to his sister's grave. What is eating you like this? No one knows. It's so miserable when Fima and I sit down opposite one another and drink vodka. You could scream. Then things get easier, but not for long. There's nowhere to go and I don't have it in me to stay. Thus we live by force of inertia. So we roll along downhill, along an inclined plane, from a mountain of recollections to a future life. Can anything really be so hopeless and grey? Can there really be no positive emotions? I don't believe it. Of course, in reality there are but, alas, they do not delight the soul. Do you remember the story of Tim Thales or the Boy who sold his Laughter? That is the name of our story too.

Surely Israel delights you. It's difficult to believe in this. Do you see, monotonous, uniform days are very different from the usual pattern of life in Odesa and, so it has turned out, devastate the soul. It is impossible to convey in words what is happening to someone going by the name of emigrant, when their native country lies thousands of kilometres behind them. And still these untamed thoughts run like yard dogs through the nooks and crannies of my consciousness, baying at me as if I were the moon, and, with each passing day, become ever more arbitrary. You want to know what Israel means to me? It's a deep blue sea, achingly blue, and a sky without a single cloud. I've only got to raise my head and Paradise, with its gates, with its eternity, with its Third Temple, becomes so clear a dream that it dumbfounds me. I can imagine what would have happened to me if I'd not lived in Israel but had been a visitor. Every visit would have been a celebration, the birth of unforgettable emotions. But each of us has our own fate, and I realise that only humility will help me to find new spiritual strength and explain how and why I came to be in the Promised Land, flowing with milk and honey. Do you and Fima have close relatives in Israel? Yes, of course, but we only communicate by phone. If we'd lived, with modern technology, we would not have spoken less, but would have met much more – at a distance we all love each other more.

Listen, yes, it's you I'm talking to. Look we're already in Jaffa. It's a long time since I did such walks. Let's continue our conversation at a café table. It's very nice here; you can smell the sea, and the creaking of yachts and the cacophony of gulls makes us more trusting and more kind. Here you forget everything; the hours, like tubs of honey, roll down the mountain of the sunset, where the flag of a victorious country joyfully encounters its traitors. You know, while mother was alive I held out, but it is six months since she left us and emptiness has settled on my heart like a desert. But I am no poet and find it difficult to convey what is going on in my soul. But why? It seems to me that if I could recount everything I feel, life would lose its meaning and I would follow mother and leave. Strange? Not at all. I'm simply sorry for Fima. He will be lost without me.

Do you often call mother to mind? Every night. How is it? Everything's fine, only it's frightening to wake up. I live for a day and it feels like an eternity. After all, you know the story of Adam. On the sixth day the Almighty created Adam; a few hours later He created Eve from his rib. Thereupon the serpent-tempter seduced Eve; they spoke, not only in words and tried the apple from the tree of good and evil, and became mortal like, indeed, us all; and on that day the Creator expelled them from Paradise, because in the Psalms of David it says a thousand years in his sight is like one day, and that is true.

How nice it is to sit with you at a table drinking white Jordanian wine, with olives and cheese, and believing in the best minutes of existence. I've put it beautifully: to sit at a table with you. But I'm actually sitting alone, whispering something to someone unknown and frightening those at neighbouring tables with my solitude and strange behaviour. Even the waiters are far from delighted with me. I'm simply interested to know which of us will pay the bill. You need not worry about that. I sorted everything out a long time ago. We're not here and this restaurant is not here, there is no Jaffa, there's nothing except the two of us. And earthly life itself has a conventional character. But enough of that. All right, they don't exist. It's more amusing like that.

What will you do when you part from me? I will live out my allotted span of days, months and years and think which of us will be the first to leave this non-existent world, Fima or me. On whom will the lot fall soonest? Although neither Fima nor I will remain alone; we will have our solitude and telephone calls; after all, our son in Canada is also alone. But why do you always go on about sad, sad things? There were certainly happy moments in life too. Tell me about them. Everything funny, unfortunately, has remained in Odesa. The customs didn't let me take them with me. Could things have turned out otherwise? What do you think? Absolutely. Do you really believe a woman can think? Forgive the tautology. Unlike men, we women do not think; we feel and live through our emotions. Cerebral activity is not for us. Although, to be serious, it might be otherwise. For my fate, and that of people like me, the Zionists are to blame. They've stirred the whole business up. They? Who? Herzl and Jabotinsky and their adherents; it was they who created the State of Israel. They hated religious Jews more than anyone. Do you have the Hasidim in mind? Precisely them. Who else? It was precisely the Orthodox Jews who thought that the creation of Israel was premature and that we had to wait for the Messiah to come and build the Third Temple and bring back all Jews from *galut*, that is to say, from exile. Even if you're at the end of the sky, I will find you and return you to Itz-Israel. Thus spake the Creator. Are you against the State of Israel then? No, of course not. You asked me if my fate could have been different and, as you realise, I expressed not my opinion, but that of all respected and honourable Hasidim. And you would like to turn time back and find yourself again in that beloved Odesa of yours? No, of course not. You Jews are a strange people.

But who are you? I am an angel. Ah! So you're not a spirit, but an angel. And if you're an angel, you're even more of a Jew. My grandmother used to tell me that the biggest antisemites were the Jews themselves. Silly me, I didn't believe her, but she really was right. Do you see, Nyusya, we angels, like humans, also come in all shapes and sizes. Yes, I'm an angel, but I'm still learning a trade. I need another two or three hundred years before I really master a trade, but it's not down to me. I'm a spiritual essence and it's much easier for me than for you human beings. I can't even imagine what would happen to me if I became human. But don't upset yourself like that – I'll feel sorry for you. You humans are remarkable beings; you must have someone to love, or at least pity. Everything is different with us. But with us humans everything is also very different.

Nyusya, time for me to go. I look forward to our next meeting. You won't believe this, but I shan't miss you. For the first time I conceived a desire to become a human. Something inexplicable has also happened to me. As in my childhood, I desperately wanted to live.

What have you done to me, angel? Don't ask. Better to release me, Nyusya.

Have I really fallen in love? What joy! I've waited for you for so long. What about Fima? I don't know, my angel, I don't know.

BERA AND CUCUMBER

Somewhere, in the wilds of the Moldavanka, under a flawless sky, where stars are scattered in summer, like leaves in autumn, there is hidden a little old Odesa courtyard, self-confident and naïve, like the dream nurtured by the Duc who has won the right to stand on Primorsky Boulevard all year round and look out to sea.

The inhabitants of this little courtyard were not especially different from the inhabitants of other courtyards, apart from this couple, mother and son. Here they are, leaving home. Let's listen to their conversation:

Mama: De Baguza de bazé?

Son: Bazé.

Mom: Be manóta chi?

Son: Útsa.

Mama: Néisyk dúkhil fo?

Son: Limatýka na koté?

Mama: Bókhil!

Son: Móza zui

Peaceful conversation smoothly switches to elevated tones.

Mama: Zóga!

Son: Gam!!

Mama: Dókha patéka?!

Son: Kótsa, kótsa!!

Mama (softly): Lákhi pu.

The mother was like a pear, a grey Bera[18] pear, the son like a cucumber, yellow and shrivelled and with purple spots, growing in a neglected vegetable patch. But before continuing to observe our heroes, I suggest we take a trip into the past and present of Odesa.

In Odesa there always have been, are, and always will be, three pleasures: the sea, the city and the courtyards. If you set off for the city you'll certainly come out at the sea. The sea is the sea – people reckon on it, earn money from it. How much? As much as they can.

The sea is affectionate, tender and defenceless in summer, prickly and irritated in winter. With its winds and the cries of gulls it lives right on the nerve ends of time, its head buried in the horizon, not wishing to acknowledge the quotidian. The sea is neither a shop window nor an aquarium. It is Rome, made by the Creator long before the appearance of Man. The sea is always expecting a lowering sky, leaden clouds, a lone figure on a deserted shore.

When speaking of the sea it is impossible not to speak of seamen. Not very long ago they were a special caste. Sailors were waited for. Sailors were loved.

The quarters to which the tourists flock and where real Odesites live are two separate towns, with feuds and nomadic raids by their core inhabitants. The first is idle and imperious, well fed, unhurried in thought and deed, the second is human and embittered, life-enhancing and gloomy, cut off from flourishing hopes by disorganisation,

....

[18]   The Beurré Bosc or Bosc is a common pear variety, originally from France or Belgium. In the Russian Empire, they were very common in the Crimea.

daily existence, screaming children and overworked streets, sickness and malaise; it yearns to earn money on the eve of running out of it. Oh, these eves – reliable and true friends of Odesites!

And finally – the courtyard. It always was the mainstay of the material and always despised the spiritual, flushing it out of the tumbledown dwellings in the same way rats are caught. And thus it always was until the Osips and Davids appeared, scraping their fiddles from morning to night. From that moment the courtyard turned into Babylon, and were it not for scandals and ladies of easy virtue, the inhabitants would die of languor and monotony.

As a rule the pitiful buildings stood in a semi-circle, and the courtyards reminded one of horseshoes, only not lucky horseshoes. You were up to your eyebrows here in good luck even without the horseshoe. The buildings stood defiantly, squashed tight against each other – oh these one-storey skyscrapers! You see, they mount an all-round defence. Against whom? First against everyone else and then against time above all.

Let's return now to our courtyard, to ask mother and son just one single question: "What is it with you? Can't you converse normally?" When I decided on this step, they were standing opposite one another like the 6 and the 12 on a clock face. My question shook them out of their equanimity and set them in motion. The mother began to move with such speed that her head was rocking like that of a Chinese porcelain idol. During this time the son would approach me, then withdraw, as if he were examining a masterpiece. I didn't know how to react. But when they joined hands and began to do a round dance around me, it seemed the earth was giving way under my feet. This went on for some ten minutes. Everything happened in complete silence.

I felt that my question was inappropriate and tactless. They didn't understand how to explain their way of life to me; this gave rise to the dance. This had just struck me when the mother began to talk in a language I knew.

"We don't think up words, we think up meanings and express them in sounds, assonances, extracting our feelings and emotions from our subconscious, and we understand one another very well. With every such dialogue our hearing becomes more refined; like a tuning fork it tunes our souls and does not force us with everyday speech into the Procrustean bed of uniform and monotonous life. Now we prepare to go out into the city as if we were setting out on a round-the-world tour. We are indefatigable romantics and which of us is Don Quixote does not matter. We are going to discover worlds which, since the time of Adam, live within us. For that we don't need much money; it's not necessary, any more than other countries and other cities."

I could see how the eyes of this elderly woman lit up, how her face was transformed. But a little distance away stood the son, smiling.

Her lips formed the shape of a final "goodbye" and again I heard the agglomeration of sounds. Their faces assumed their former masks and they set off unhurriedly for the city in search of Dulcinea.

CHALIK AND GELIK

Chalik had done Gelik a mischief. Not that Gelik was upset; he simply felt out of sorts. All the same, they'd mucked about together for so many years that this was neither here nor there. "Well, what is there to whinge about?" thought Gelik and followed his nose home. When Gloza, Gelik's wife, saw her dreamy better half, she guessed at once what sort of a dog's breakfast her shambolic man had made of things.

"I warned you, you airhead, but you only listened to your mate and now you've got what you deserved – a prob. The more so because it's not the first time Chalik has fetched you one up the bracket. What more can I say – you'd better go and see to the sprogs. Your beloved Blyunya has been sitting on the pot for three days, like the princess and the pea, and that's with a king daddy like you, *azohen vey.*"

Gelik flexed his legs and set off in the direction of Blyunya. At that moment the elder Chmotsyk arrived, asked for some nosh and something to follow. Gloza's peepers were on stalks and she at once gave him a third course, so he didn't blag anything else before supper. Everything would have been OK if Bukhtya, Gloza's mother, had not overheard her daughter's conversation with this loser.

"How long can you keep this misery-guts in the house? He should have slung his hook a long time ago. But no, you weren't satisfied with one Chmotsyk, you had to have Blyunya as well. So go and knock about with those kids, but where do I fit in?"

"Mum, you never do fit in. I don't remember that tosser, my dad, and how often he drank your blood and managed some of mine too. So, mum, let's not lose our rag, let's let everything go while it's worth it. Life's not as soft as you took it into your thick skull to think. Do something a bit simpler. Tidy the house up at last or get on the nerves of Putsyk, our neighbour. After all, you're good at that."

"Give over, Gloza! You always change the subject and I don't like it."

"Mum, who knows what we like when we feel sick."

"Maybe you're right, but I want some peace!"

"Mum, don't hurry, he'll soon be here anyway."

Time was moving casually towards the sunset. It was time for everyone to gather round the round table and talk about something nice.

"How much of that is possible, about nothing at all?" Gloza thought, whereupon, in front of everyone, she picked up Blyunya, took her in her arms, kissed her mother, put her head on Gelik's shoulder and burst into tears. All the same, what a joy it is to have children, a concerned husband, a kind mother and a friend like Chalik! Maybe he's wrong, but in his own way. Maybe he knows better. And the fact that we are often in debt to him and don't pay up – who doesn't that happen to?

HAIFA

The events of which I want to speak took place on 9 May 1996.

Dad was seriously ill. He spent his whole time in an armchair, reading his newspaper, his face emaciated with illness.

Every ninth of May Dad was transformed, and this day was no exception, despite his failing health. For people who had lived through and survived the terrible Second World War, it was a special day.

From early morning on, Dad felt incredibly anxious, and his agitation conveyed itself to us. We rushed and bustled about, trying somehow to match Dad's mood. He meanwhile, summoning up his strength, like a ship's captain coming onto dry land, got out of his armchair and occupied himself with mundane matters. First, Dad would get his dress uniform, with its medals, out of the cupboard, then he would put it back again. While so doing he would find time to grumble and to be extremely displeased with us, thinking that we were doing everything wrong on that day. What exactly we were doing wrong, no one knew. But Dad kept repeating: "You just don't understand. Today is a big holiday!" He would raise his right hand in military fashion, denoting that this event had special status.

On that day Dad paid particular attention to ironing his trousers. He did not entrust this important task to anyone.

He would put a damp cloth over his miserable, shrivelled trousers and iron them until they lost consciousness, so that the stripes, reminiscent of war-wound scars, ran the whole length of the trouser legs. An incredible cloud of steam hung round Dad, making him almost invisible, but when the flogging of the trousers was over, the vapour dissipated and Dad came back to us, like the High Priest from the Temple after the prayers for Yom Kippur. Then, with a feeling of duty done he set off for the harbour, to wit, his armchair, and dozed off. We went about on tiptoe, so as not to disturb his rest at any price.

Suddenly Dad opened his eyes and said: "Son, this evening take me to Haifa. After all today is my day." I was baffled and did not know what to say in reply, but Dad was relentless: "Do you realise, son, that to this day I can't forget the day when I was there with the Hasidim from America." I was uneasy; after all Dad had never been to Israel. I exchanged glances with my wife, Lyuda. Could Dad be delirious? A few minutes later, with a note of hurt in his voice, Dad asked: "Son, is it hard for you to book a table in the Haifa restaurant in Podil?" Then he gave a deep sigh and added: "Maybe you don't know I've got a bit left." I felt terribly embarrassed. How had I failed to realise that he wasn't talking about Israel but about the Haifa restaurant in Kyiv? At once I felt easier. In Dad's presence I at once booked a table for that evening and invited our friends Seryozha and Tanya Polyakov to mark the day with us, since their father had also gone through the whole war, ending up as a colonel.

In the evening Dad summoned up his strength; we ordered a taxi and arrived at the restaurant together with our friends. Apart from us there was not a soul in the restaurant. We sat at the guest table, raised glasses of vodka to the Victory and to Dad's good health. We were already getting ready to leave when a noise erupted in the restaurant and there came the sound of many people talking in an incomprehensible language.

In a matter of minutes the whole restaurant was filled with Hasidim. The waiters quickly moved all the restaurant tables aside and the newcomers occupied one large table alongside us. The Hasidim were incredibly noisy and cheerful, and when they began to sing, Dad was transformed. Not a trace of his illness remained. One of the rabbis recognised Dad and their joy knew no bounds. They at once invited Dad to their table and for a whole two hours they sang songs, both in Yiddish and Hebrew. Dad was happy, and we with him.

A month later Dad passed away.

SON

Silence shortens distance. We find one another. The birds are singing, not only in my garden, but in yours too. Once upon a time we had one garden for the two of us. Now we've become richer. Each of us has his own garden. The tops of my trees rest against the sky, and yours go through it with their roots.

What has changed round about? Nothing. There are always people somewhere; even as a child, you often went away, and we missed you and waited. Now we don't wait. Before, we were offended. Now we are not. I wanted to say: "You remember," but I won't.

Memories make us even more lonely. We become like trees in winter. I look at their bare flesh, shyly avert my gaze and don't know where to put myself or what to do with this cloud called soul.

My memory stands behind your back, you are frying sunflower seeds in a hot frying pan, carefully sprinkling them with salt with a tablespoon, and stirring them unhurriedly. I come a bit nearer, you feel my breath, and, as if nothing has happened: "Son, I'll just finish frying them, they can cool down a bit and we'll go to the football. There's still time."

There is always time, but not always us. It's not only that you've aged. "Don't talk about that." "Yes, you're right. I mustn't."

Everyone has their own way of denying what is happening. Yours is in the present, mine in the past. Events, like raindrops, have not yet appeared before they disappear and dissolve in our consciousness, but our heartbeat keeps us afloat and we, like goose-quill floats, leave ripples on the water of life.

Papa, when you're not with me on earth, I will be with you in heaven.

ABOUT THE TRANSLATOR

Michael Pursglove (born 22 September 1944) is a retired Senior Lecturer in Modern Languages at Exeter University. He was educated at Bradford Grammar School, King's College Cambridge and New College, Oxford. He also taught at the universities of Ulster, Reading and Bath. He has published, as translator or co-translator, eleven book-length translations, including five novels and a volume of short stories by Turgenev and, most recently, the Ukrainian novels *Children of Grad*, O *Venice*, and Alexander Korotko's *Moon Boy*. He has also written widely on literature and translation issues, most recently in *East-West Review*. His published translations of poetry include works by Pushkin, Lermontov, Turgenev, Akhmatova and Mandelshtam.

WAR POEMS

by Alexander Korotko

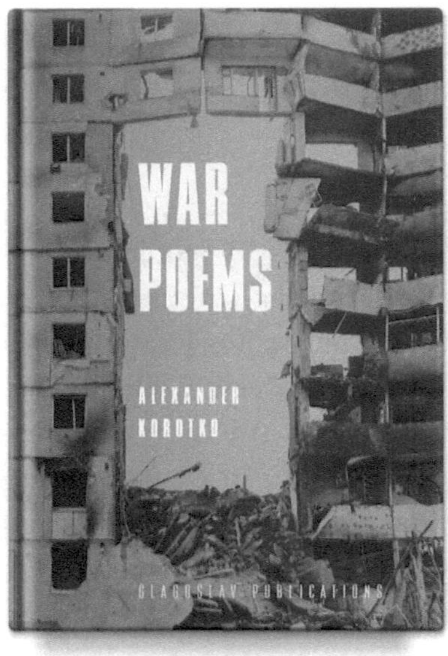

Soon after Russia invaded Ukraine on 24th February 2022, author and poet Alexander Korotko began to set down as poetry the turbulent responses at the emotional, philosophical and simply human levels evoked by the resulting war. Thus, we read in the 88 poems in this volume – completed in just less than 100 days – of the seemingly endless wail of sirens; of sheltering in cellars and tunnels; of the celebrated Ukrainian steppe, churned by tanks; the dead – "our killed, have become our Saviour Angels"; and whole poems devoted to Irpin and Mariupol as the atrocities there and elsewhere became known. Korotko is not without compassion for the Russian soldier – "Russian soldier, what did you forget in my land? We had grief enough without you." – and the soldier's mother when she receives his dead body as "cargo 200". Neither does he conceal his frustration with Ukraine's allies – "we pay the West for help with blood, but the West makes no haste to deliver."

Buy it > www.glagoslav.com

THE VILLAGE TEACHER AND OTHER STORIES

by Theodore Odrach

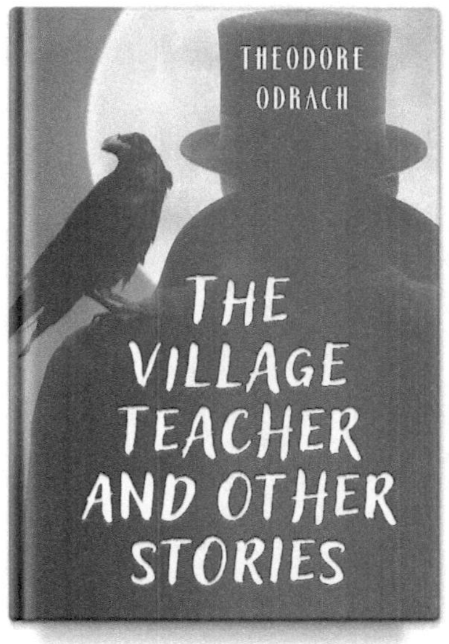

The twenty-two stories in this collection, set mostly in Eastern Europe during World War Two, depict a world fraught with conflict and chaos. Theodore Odrach is witness to the horrors that surround him, and as both an investigative journalist and a skilful storyteller, using humor and irony, he guides us through his remarkable narratives. His writing style is clean and spare, yet at the same time compelling and complex. There is no short supply of triumph and catastrophe, courage and cowardice, good and evil, as they impact the lives of ordinary people.

In "Benny's Story", a group of prisoners fight to survive despite horrific circumstances; in "Lickspittles", the absurdity of an émigré writer's life is highlighted; in "Blood", a young man travels to a distant city in search of his lost love; in "Whistle Stop", two German soldiers fight boredom in an out-of-the-way outpost, only to see their world crumble and fall.

Buy it > www.glagoslav.com

ABSOLUTE ZERO

by Artem Chekh

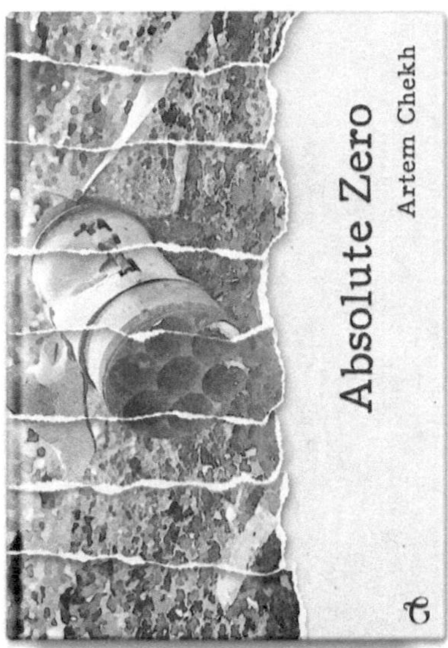

The book is a first person account of a soldier's journey, and is based on Artem Chekh's diary that he wrote while and after his service in the war in Donbas. One of the most important messages the book conveys is that war means pain. Chekh is not showing the reader any heroic combat, focusing instead on the quiet, mundane, and harsh soldier's life. Chekh masterfully selects the most poignant details of this kind of life.

Artem Chekh (1985) is a contemporary Ukrainian writer, author of more than ten books of fiction and essays. *Absolute Zero* (2017), an account of Chekh's service in the army in the war in Donbas, is one of his latest books, for which he became a recipient of several prestigious awards in Ukraine, such as the Joseph Conrad Prize (2019), the Gogol Prize (2018), the Voyin Svitla (2018), and the Litaktsent Prize (2017). This is his first book-length translation into English.

Buy it > www.glagoslav.com

THE FANTASTIC WORLDS OF YURI VYNNYCHUK

by Yuri Vynnychuk

Yuri Vynnychuk is a master storyteller and satirist, who emerged from the Western Ukrainian underground in Soviet times to become one of Ukraine's most prolific and most prominent writers of today. He is a chameleon who can adapt his narrative voice in a variety of ways and whose style at times is reminiscent of Borges. A master of the short story, he exhibits a great range from exquisite lyrical-philosophical works such as his masterpiece "An Embroidered World," written in the mode of magical realism; to intense psychological studies; to contemplative science fiction and horror tales; and to wicked black humor and satire such as his "Max and Me." Excerpts are also presented in this volume of his longer prose works, including his highly acclaimed novel of wartime Lviv *Tango of Death*, which received the 2012 BBC Ukrainian Book of the Year Award. The translations offered here allow the English-language reader to become acquainted with the many fantastic worlds and lyrical imagination of an extraordinarily versatile writer.

Buy it > www.glagoslav.com

OLANDA

by Rafał Wojasiński

I've been happy since the morning. Delighted, even. Everything seems so splendidly transient to me. That dust, from which thou art and unto which thou shalt return — it tempts me. And that's why I wander about these roads, these woods, among the nearby houses, from which waft the aromas of fried pork chops, chicken soup, fish, diapers, steamed potatoes for the pigs; I lose my eye-sight, and regain it again. I don't know what life is, Ola, but I'm holding on to it. Thus speaks the narrator of Rafał Wojasiński's novel Olanda. Awarded the prestigious Marek Nowakowski Prize for 2019, *Olanda* introduces us to a world we glimpse only through the window of our train, as we hurry from one important city to another: a provincial world of dilapidated farmhouses and sagging apartment blocks, overgrown cemeteries and village drunks; a world seemingly abandoned by God — and yet full of the basic human joy of life itself.

Ravens before Noah

by Susanna Harutyunyan

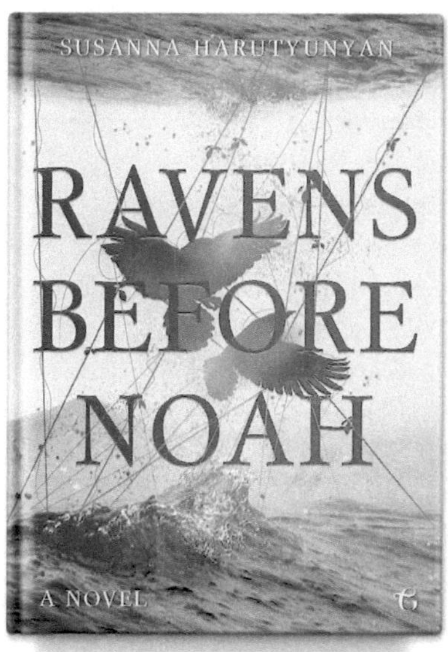

This novel is set in the Armenian mountains sometime in 1915-1960. An old man and a new born baby boy escape from the Hamidian massacres in Turkey in 1894 and hide themselves in the ruins of a demolished and abandoned village. The village soon becomes a shelter for many others, who flee from problems with the law, their families, or their past lives. The villagers survive in this secret shelter, cut off from the rest of the world, by selling or bartering their agricultural products in the villages beneath the mountain.

Years pass by, and the child saved by the old man grows into a young man, Harout. He falls for a beautiful girl who arrived in the village after being tortured by Turkish soldiers. She is pregnant and the old women of the village want to kill the twin baby girls as soon as they are born, to wash away the shame…

Buy it > www.glagoslav.com

- *A History of Belarus* by Lubov Bazan
- *Children's Fashion of the Russian Empire* by Alexander Vasiliev
- *Empire of Corruption: The Russian National Pastime* by Vladimir Soloviev
- *Heroes of the 90s: People and Money. The Modern History of Russian Capitalism* by Alexander Solovev, Vladislav Dorofeev and Valeria Bashkirova
- *Fifty Highlights from the Russian Literature* (Dutch Edition) by Maarten Tengbergen
- *Bajesvolk* (Dutch Edition) by Michail Chodorkovsky
- *Dagboek van Keizerin Alexandra* (Dutch Edition)
- *Myths about Russia* by Vladimir Medinskiy
- *Boris Yeltsin: The Decade that Shook the World* by Boris Minaev
- *A Man Of Change: A study of the political life of Boris Yeltsin*
- *Sberbank: The Rebirth of Russia's Financial Giant* by Evgeny Karasyuk
- *To Get Ukraine* by Oleksandr Shyshko
- *Asystole* by Oleg Pavlov
- *Gnedich* by Maria Rybakova
- *Marina Tsvetaeva: The Essential Poetry*
- *Multiple Personalities* by Tatyana Shcherbina
- *The Investigator* by Margarita Khemlin
- *The Exile* by Zinaida Tulub
- *Leo Tolstoy: Flight from Paradise* by Pavel Basinsky
- *Moscow in the 1930* by Natalia Gromova
- *Laurus* (Dutch edition) by Evgenij Vodolazkin
- *Prisoner* by Anna Nemzer
- *The Crime of Chernobyl: The Nuclear Goulag* by Wladimir Tchertkoff
- *Alpine Ballad* by Vasil Bykau
- *The Complete Correspondence of Hryhory Skovoroda*
- *The Tale of Aypi* by Ak Welsapar
- *Selected Poems* by Lydia Grigorieva
- *The Fantastic Worlds of Yuri Vynnychuk*
- *The Garden of Divine Songs and Collected Poetry of Hryhory Skovoroda*
- *Adventures in the Slavic Kitchen: A Book of Essays with Recipes* by Igor Klekh
- *Seven Signs of the Lion* by Michael M. Naydan

- *Forefathers' Eve* by Adam Mickiewicz
- *One-Two* by Igor Eliseev
- *Girls, be Good* by Bojan Babić
- *Time of the Octopus* by Anatoly Kucherena
- *The Grand Harmony* by Bohdan Ihor Antonych
- *The Selected Lyric Poetry Of Maksym Rylsky*
- *The Shining Light* by Galymkair Mutanov
- *The Frontier: 28 Contemporary Ukrainian Poets - An Anthology*
- *Acropolis: The Wawel Plays* by Stanisław Wyspiański
- *Contours of the City* by Attyla Mohylny
- *Conversations Before Silence: The Selected Poetry of Oles Ilchenko*
- *The Secret History of my Sojourn in Russia* by Jaroslav Hašek
- *Mirror Sand: An Anthology of Russian Short Poems*
- *Maybe We're Leaving* by Jan Balaban
- *Death of the Snake Catcher* by Ak Welsapar
- *A Brown Man in Russia* by Vijay Menon
- *Hard Times* by Ostap Vyshnia
- *The Flying Dutchman* by Anatoly Kudryavitsky
- *Nikolai Gumilev's Africa* by Nikolai Gumilev
- *Combustions* by Srđan Srdić
- *The Sonnets* by Adam Mickiewicz
- *Dramatic Works* by Zygmunt Krasiński
- *Four Plays* by Juliusz Słowacki
- *Little Zinnobers* by Elena Chizhova
- *We Are Building Capitalism! Moscow in Transition 1992-1997* by Robert Stephenson
- *The Nuremberg Trials* by Alexander Zvyagintsev
- *The Hemingway Game* by Evgeni Grishkovets
- *A Flame Out at Sea* by Dmitry Novikov
- *Jesus' Cat* by Grig
- *Want a Baby and Other Plays* by Sergei Tretyakov
- *Mikhail Bulgakov: The Life and Times* by Marietta Chudakova
- *Leonardo's Handwriting* by Dina Rubina
- *A Burglar of the Better Sort* by Tytus Czyżewski
- *The Mouseiad and other Mock Epics* by Ignacy Krasicki

- *Ravens before Noah* by Susanna Harutyunyan
- *An English Queen and Stalingrad* by Natalia Kulishenko
- *Point Zero* by Narek Malian
- *Absolute Zero* by Artem Chekh
- *Olanda* by Rafał Wojasiński
- *Robinsons* by Aram Pachyan
- *The Monastery* by Zakhar Prilepin
- *The Selected Poetry of Bohdan Rubchak: Songs of Love, Songs of Death, Songs of the Moon*
- *Mebet* by Alexander Grigorenko
- *The Orchestra* by Vladimir Gonik
- *Everyday Stories* by Mima Mihajlović
- *Slavdom* by Ľudovít Štúr
- *The Code of Civilization* by Vyacheslav Nikonov
- *Where Was the Angel Going?* by Jan Balaban
- *De Zwarte Kip* (Dutch Edition) by Antoni Pogorelski
- *Głosy / Voices* by Jan Polkowski
- *Sergei Tretyakov: A Revolutionary Writer in Stalin's Russia* by Robert Leach
- *Opstand* (Dutch Edition) by Władysław Reymont
- *Dramatic Works* by Cyprian Kamil Norwid
- *Children's First Book of Chess* by Natalie Shevando and Matthew McMillion
- *Precursor* by Vasyl Shevchuk
- *The Vow: A Requiem for the Fifties* by Jiří Kratochvil
- *De Bibliothecaris* (Dutch edition) by Mikhail Jelizarov
- *Subterranean Fire* by Natalka Bilotserkivets
- *Vladimir Vysotsky: Selected Works*
- *Behind the Silk Curtain* by Gulistan Khamzayeva
- *The Village Teacher and Other Stories* by Theodore Odrach
- *Duel* by Borys Antonenko-Davydovych
- *War Poems* by Alexander Korotko
- *Ballads and Romances* by Adam Mickiewicz
- *The Revolt of the Animals* by Wladyslaw Reymont
- *Poems about my Psychiatrist* by Andrzej Kotański
- *Someone Else's Life* by Elena Dolgopyat
- *Selected Works: Poetry, Drama, Prose* by Jan Kochanowski

- *The Riven Heart of Moscow (Sivtsev Vrazhek)* by Mikhail Osorgin
- *Bera and Cucumber* by Alexander Korotko
- *The Big Fellow* by Anastasiia Marsiz
- *Liza's Waterfall: The Hidden Story of a Russian Feminist* by Pavel Basinsky
- *Biography of Sergei Prokofiev* by Igor Vishnevetsky
- *Ilget* by Alexander Grigorenko
- *A City Drawn from Memory* by Elena Chizhova
- *Guide to M. Bulgakov's The Master and Margarita* by Ksenia Atarova and Georgy Lesskis

More to come . . .

GLAGOSLAV PUBLICATIONS
www.glagoslav.com